THE BLUE HELMET

THE BLUE HELMET

a novel

WILLIAM BELL

DOUBLEDAY CANADA

Doubleday Canada and colophon are trademarks.

LIBRARY AND ARCHIVES CANADA CATALOGUING IN PUBLICATION

Bell, William, 1945–
The blue helmet / William Bell.

ISBN-13: 978-0-385-66246-8
ISBN-10: 0-385-66246-7

I. Title.

PS8553.E4568B58 2006 jC813'.54 C2006-901454-X

Jacket map: Central Intelligence Agency
Printed and bound in the USA

Published in Canada by
Doubleday Canada, a division of
Random House of Canada Limited

Visit Random House of Canada Limited's website:
www.randomhouse.ca

BVG 10 9 8 7 6 5 4 3 2 1

For Reg Lashbrook

PART ONE

LEE

What god was it, then, set them
together in bitter collision?

—Homer, *The Iliad*

ONE

"I THOUGHT YOU GUYS aren't supposed to smoke on duty."

The fat plainclothes cop named Carpino lowered his window an inch.

"You're a strange one to talk about rules," he said.

The unmarked police car hissed through deserted Sunday morning streets, wipers flapping greasy drizzle from the windshield, the rattling fan fighting a losing battle against condensation. My father would have had a fit if he'd heard the fan, and launched into a rant about proper maintenance. But, as usual, he wasn't around.

I sat up front beside the cop. The car was hot and stuffy and smelled of stale coffee, hamburger grease, and tobacco. With the palm of my hand I squeegeed mist from the side window. Outside, the rain brimmed in the curb gutters, pushing dirt and soggy food wrappers toward plugged sewer grates.

My head throbbed and I winced every time the car hit a pothole. I flipped down the visor and examined my face in the vanity mirror. An angry red scab was forming over the split in my swollen upper lip, my nose was puffed and red, and the cheek under one eye was bruised and purple. Disgusted, I pushed the visor back into position.

"Anyway," I told the cop, "you're wasting your time. I'll be back."

He dropped his cigarette butt out the window, took a left through an orange light, and headed toward the on-ramp for the highway.

"Think about it, Lee," he replied. "You've got no choice here. You've burned all your bridges."

I said nothing. Maybe he was right, maybe he wasn't. I stared out the side window and let my mind take me back to the night before, to my assignment. I played the scene over and over, searching for clues that would tell me what had gone wrong.

"It'll be a piece of cake."

"I've heard that one before."

"No, really. You'll be in and out in five minutes, ten at the most."

Classes were in session and the school parking lot was quiet. I was supposed to be in Math class.

"Where is this place?" I asked, zipping my jacket against the frosty breeze.

Vernor opened the driver's door of his Mustang and pulled a folded map from the door pocket. He spread the map on the hood, tapped a spot with a finger tip.

"Here. On Market Street."

"Down by the docks. Near the old distillery."

"Right. You get around back through the alley. It's an auto supply store, a small one, with an office on the second floor."

"So it'll have a burglar alarm."

"My source says not. Here's how it will work. Behind the store, there's a small basement window, almost hidden by a dumpster. It's broken. You go in, make your way to the second floor. Leave through the back door and down the fire escape. You make sure the door is left unlocked."

"And then what?"

"And then nothing. You just walk away. We'll take care of the rest."

"What's in there? Cash?"

"Not for you to know."

"Why don't I just take what you want while I'm there?"

"Not for you to know."

"What's the point of me going in through the window and leaving the door unlocked if—"

"You ask too many questions. That's always been your problem."

A gust of wind snatched the map and Vernor lunged to recapture it. He folded it, pushed long, black hair out of his eyes. "This is your last initiation test. Do it right and I won't say anything about you letting that grade nine kid off the hook. You'll get your patch. You'll be a Tarantula."

As he spoke he opened the front of his denim jacket a little, revealing a small yellow square with a black spider stitched onto it. When the jacket was done up, the tarantula would rest on his heart.

"When?" I asked.

"It has to be tonight. After midnight."

"Consider it done," I said.

"Don't screw up," he warned, then climbed into the Mustang and peeled out of the parking lot.

The Tarantulas were the best gang in my neighbourhood—the biggest, the most powerful—and if you belonged you didn't need to worry about anything. They took care of their own. You always had a place to go, someone to turn to. Nobody crossed a Tarantula without the whole crew coming after him.

But it was hard to get in. There were tests to prove your obedience and allegiance, and if you passed you were a member for life. "Like being a Catholic," Vernor had joked when he was explaining things to me. "You're expected to return loyalty with loyalty. No exceptions. And you follow orders, even if you don't like them. Sometimes you gotta do things you don't want to, but when the shit flies, you got the whole outfit behind you. You're never alone. It's like the army."

TWO

IT WAS RAINING WHEN I got to Market Street, and I
was numb with cold from my bike ride across town. Teeth
chattering, I cruised along the deserted, oily-wet street,
steering around potholes and squinting into the dark. The
auto parts store was squeezed into the gloom between a
decrepit warehouse and the gigantic bulk of the old distillery. A battered Ford slumped at the curb, its hood up, its
windows smashed, its wheels long gone. A dented hot dog
vendor's cart lay on its side under one of the few unbroken
street lights.

At the end of the block I turned, retraced my route,
and rode into the inky dark of the alley, struck by the
rank odour of cat piss and motor oil. I decided to leave
the bike a few feet in from the street rather than take it
farther and risk puncturing the tires on a nail or broken
glass.

The dumpster was parked up against the back wall of the store, leaving a narrow gap, and the basement window was broken, just like Vernor had said. I was in and out in no time. At the bottom of the fire escape, I scanned the dark lane for any sign of movement, then stole along the back of the store. The far end of the alley was a lighter shade of dark, where I should have seen the silhouette of my bike.

It wasn't there.

I dashed down the alley and into the street—and smashed into something that lit up a ball of blinding white fire behind my eyes. I felt my nose crack before I collapsed. Heard my skull thump on the sidewalk. I was hauled to my feet and slammed against the bricks. I slid down the wall, head spinning. A hand jammed under my chin, clutched the neck of my jacket and hoisted me up. Another hand frisked me and jerked my wallet out of my back pocket.

The mugger let go and I slumped to the wet pavement again. Icy water seeped through my jeans. The lights in my head dimmed. Something wet trickled down the back of my neck. Something salty oozed into my mouth. I forced my eyes open, tried to focus. A bulky shape crouched in front of me and a sandpapery voice ordered, "Get up."

I struggled to my feet, one hand on the wall like a drunk, spat out a stream of blood. I blinked. The bulk became a broad-shouldered man in a long open coat. Beside him was a tall cop holding a nightstick. It was the nightstick, I guessed, that had bloodied my nose.

"Ah, shit," the one wearing the overcoat growled. "False alarm. He's just a kid. Take him in and book him."

He turned and headed toward a car parked cockeyed against the curb. His companion stepped in front of me, a plastic rain shield on his cap, a gun riding on one hip. He held my wallet up to the light, squinting.

"You're Lee Mercer?"

Before I could answer the other cop spun on his heel. "What was that?" he called out.

"School ID card says Lee Mercer," the uniform answered. "You know him?"

The plainclothes cop snatched the ID and examined it. "You Doug Mercer's kid?"

"None of your friggin' business."

A stinging slap snapped my head back. "Let's try again," he said, almost whispering, his voice flat. "Are you Doug's kid?"

"What if I am?"

"Gimme his ID. I'll take it from here," he said to the uniform. "Impound the bike."

THREE

"GOT AN EMPTY INTERVIEW room, Manny?" the cop said to the uniform behind the long desk at the police station. Around me, unhappy people shouted, cried, argued.

The uniform looked me up and down. "Evenin' Marchi," he replied. He consulted a book. "Number three is guest-free at the moment."

"This one's unofficial for the time being," Marchi said.

He pushed me down a corridor, threw open a door, and shoved me inside. A table and three chairs sat under a garish ceiling light.

"Sit," he ordered.

I did as he said. He reached behind him, came up with a pair of handcuffs, snapped one ring around my wrist and the other around a table leg.

"Don't go anywhere," he said and left, slamming the door.

A shiver ran down my back. The room was warm, but my clothes and hair were still soaking wet from the rain. With my free hand, I felt the back of my head. Blood came away on my fingers. My nostrils were plugged with blood, too. I blew them clear and winced from the pain, wiped my hand on my pant leg.

I looked toward the mirror on the opposite wall, did my best to offer a sneer in case someone was watching from the other side. I settled back, got as comfortable as I could with my arm shackled to the table leg, and waited.

"Jesus," my father groaned, shaking his head. "Look at you. What the hell have you done this time?"

Marchi the cop had come back to the interview room hours later and driven me across town through the rainy dawn to the apartment house where I lived with my father. He hadn't said a word during the trip. At our door he had shaken hands with my father and followed me inside.

"What do you care?" I answered.

"Now, look—"

Marchi had held up his hand as if directing traffic. "Later, fellas. I gotta get a load off my feet, okay? Why doesn't Lee get cleaned up and you and me can discuss the situation," he suggested.

While I showered and changed my clothes I heard them talking in the living room. It was only when I returned that I noticed a suitcase beside the door.

"Sit down, Lee," the cop said.

I stood where I was and looked at my father. He was wearing his coveralls, ready for work at the auto shop a few blocks away. His dark hair was combed straight back, his face pale and drawn, and he had his What-am-I-going-to-do-with-you look on. He nodded toward the couch.

"Do like Marchi says, Lee."

The cop sat on the edge of the ottoman beside my father's tattered easy chair, so I was facing the two of them like in an interview. Marchi still had his overcoat on, with a chequered sports jacket underneath.

"Lee," my father began, working hard to keep his voice steady, "this is Sergeant Marchi Carpino. He's a friend from way back. He was good enough to call me after he picked you up. Thanks to him, you haven't been arrested."

"Thanks to him my nose is probably broken," I said.

My father ground a fist into his palm. "I've just about reached the end of my rope. I'm scared that if you go on like this you'll end up in jail. So I've made a decision."

He paused, as if psyching himself up, and took a deep breath, locking eyes with me. "You're going to New Toronto to live with your Aunt Reena," he said. "I called her last night after I heard from Marchi. You—"

"I'm not go—"

My father shot out of his chair, pale with rage. "Shut up!" he shouted. "Just shut the hell up! I've had enough!" He hung his head, breathing deeply, sat back down. When he had regained control he said, "Lee, you're going and that's all there is to it. Marchi will explain things on the way."

Marchi stood, walked to the door, and picked up the suitcase. "Do I need to cuff you?"

I looked at my father. He returned my stare, his eyes flinty with determination.

"No," I said to the cop. "I got nowhere to run."

_____

Carpino took the on-ramp and merged into the traffic on the Queen Elizabeth Way. As we headed east the rain let up and the swarm of cars, trucks and buses bunched tighter. Carpino fumbled his pack of cigarettes from inside his pocket. "You feel like listening now?" he asked.

"Do I have a choice?"

"See?" he said, lighting up, "that kind of smart-ass talk indicates that the answer to my question is no. Trouble is, I gotta explain some things to you before I drop you off. But first you gotta open your ears."

I stared at the floor. Between my feet, an empty paper cup rolled back and forth.

"So, talk."

"Your father wants you to live with your aunt for a while—"

"Yeah, well, soon as you drop me off, I'm out of there—"

"—and I figured I should explain things real clear so you don't do what you just said you were going to do. You want a cigarette?"

"Don't smoke."

"One for the plus side. Anyway, here's the thing. You've been suspended from school twice, for fighting. The Board of Ed told your dad that next time you're expelled for good—"

"I don't give a—"

"—and I'm pretty sure you're behind a couple of assaults that happened near your school. It's only a matter of time before we can hang them on you. When that happens, you're not a naughty boy fighting in the schoolyard any more. You'll go into custody. Believe me, you don't want that."

I kept my mouth shut. There were three assaults, not two, if you counted the grade nine kid I grabbed and shook without working him over like I was supposed to do. He was so terrified I thought he was going to piss himself. Vernor hadn't been too happy when he found out I let the kid go with a warning.

As we passed the junction with highway 427, Carpino eased the car into the collector lanes. By now the traffic was moving slowly—people heading downtown to work. Carpino took the turnoff for 18th Street and pulled up at a traffic light.

He lit a fresh cigarette off the butt of the old one and took up his lecture. "Besides the assaults, we got you for break and enter. Throw in resisting arrest and we'll have you eating institution food until well past your best-before date."

"Bullshit. I'll get off," I said, with more confidence than I felt. I didn't know much about the legal system. "I got no record. I'm a young offender."

"That one's easy. Lee. We nail you for one of the assaults. You go to court, get let off by some kindly but stupid judge like you said, but then you'll have a record. We pick you up for the other assaults and the burglary. Then you go inside."

He braked and steered into a parking lot behind a small hotel and turned off the motor. "Now, I hope you're clear on your situation, Lee. If I have to arrest you, I'll throw the book at you, like they say in the TV cop shows. If you stay here with your aunt," he nodded toward a door in the building across the street, "I let you alone. There's nobody to go back to anyway, except your dad, and he's not happy with you right now."

"I don't need him," I spat. "I got my friends."

"Who? The Tarantulas?"

"Yeah, the Tarantulas. At least they got some loyalty."

He ran the window down a few inches and tossed the butt out. "Haven't you figured out why we were waiting for you when you jumped off the fire escape? We'd been investigating a series of burglaries in the area—offices, warehouses, all small concerns without much security. We got a call, tipping us off that the auto parts store was going to be hit."

Carpino rolled the window back up and turned toward me, his eyes hard. "Think about this," he said. "Who knew you were going to break into that place?"

I didn't remember my aunt very well. She wasn't around when I was a kid. But I had stayed with her once before, when my mother was dying.

Mom was diagnosed with terminal cancer when I was seven. She was an art lover and a painter whose unframed landscapes were tacked up all over our apartment. My father wanted to take her to Italy before she died— although he never put it in those words—because she had always dreamed of visiting Rome and Venice and Florence to feast on paintings and sculptures. I remember the discussions and arguments Mom and Dad had—about the expense, about maybe taking me with them—before they finally packed me up and drove me to my aunt's, promising they'd come home soon and bring me lots of presents.

When they returned, she was pale and weak. She had lost weight, but her eyes were bright with excitement, and she began a new painting the same day. Before she was able to finish it, an ambulance carried her off to the hospital. They hooked her up with wires and tubes, and her body under the bed sheet was like the stick-figures I drew at school.

She never came home. One afternoon my father sat me down in the kitchen and crouched before me, holding my hands, and told me in a voice he could barely control to pretend she was on another trip and that we'd see her again some day. Even at seven, I was too old for that crap. I was confused and terrified, but I knew my mother wasn't on holiday.

I hardly saw my father after that. He held two jobs, the auto repair during the day, a department store at nights and on Saturdays. Neither one paid a decent wage. He was gone when I got up in the morning and never home before ten at night, when he'd drag himself into the apartment, eat, have a few beers, and fall asleep in front of the TV. When I was little, baby-sitters looked after me Saturdays and after school. When I got older, I took care of myself.

For a long time I thought he was burying himself in work because he missed my mom. Then one day I realized it was more than that. He was paying back the thousands he had borrowed so he could take her to Italy. From the age of seven I grew up without parents. One was dead, one was a zombie who hardly spoke to me, who I often felt blamed me in some way for his wife's deadly illness. Which was funny, because for a long time I blamed him.

I spent most of my life alone, without much help when my eyes dimmed from the dark rage that took hold of me and scared the hell out of me because I didn't know what it was or how to deal with it.

FOUR

"You smell like onions."

"How's it going, Your Majesty?" I said to the old woman beside me.

I poured myself a coffee and replaced the pot on the hot-plate under a sign that said

HELP YOURSELF

COFFEE $1

WITH MILK &/OR SUGAR, $1.50

"If people want to ruin good Colombian," Reena had told me more than a month ago when she showed me around Reena's Unique Café for the first time, "they'll have to pay for the privilege."

I called the old lady "Your Majesty" because she spent all day circling the block, pushing a grocery cart piled high with her belongings and calling out, "I am the Queen of Sweden!" Rain or shine, she wore a long knitted scarf, striped blue and gold, and a dirty white toque. Where she slept at night, I had no idea—probably in the big park across the road.

"You smell like onions," she repeated, dumping another spoonful of sugar into her coffee and stirring as if she was punishing it. "And your eyes are red."

"Been slicing in the kitchen. For the soup of the day."

"You work here?" she asked.

"Yeah. Chief busboy and onion chopper-upper."

"Do you like it?"

"Not really, but I don't have much choice."

"Reena never mentioned you," she said, and shuffled off to a table.

The Queen and I had had the same conversation half a dozen times. Her memory seemed to come and go, but she remembered to turn up at the café almost every morning.

A few more street people, their faces pale, their clothes tattered, sat around the tables Reena kept at the back of the small restaurant, drinking coffee and staring into a personal nowhere. Reena let them have the coffee—and cookies, if she had any around—for nothing, as long as they were quiet and didn't stay too long. She had a soft spot for people who floated on the edge of the stream, which is why she had taken me in.

Reena had given me the room on the third floor, up a narrow flight of creaky stairs from her apartment. There was space for a bed, a night table that was really an upended wooden box, an easy chair that was older than me, and one of those rugs made from one piece of material that spiralled out from the centre. No TV. No sound system, unless you counted the digital clock radio that read 10:00 a.m. all day. The ancient radiator thumped and gurgled at night.

I had my own bathroom with a shower, and the room was bright. The front window looked out over Lakeshore Boulevard and the park. If I craned my neck, I could glimpse the lake. From the side window I could see 18th Street and the run-down hotel where Carpino had parked the day he delivered me to Reena. It was an okay place to stay until I figured out my next move.

I carried my coffee to the booth nearest the counter. It was one of five that Reena had kept when she renovated the place a few years before. Why she hung onto them, she never explained. They were covered in red vinyl pimpled by cigarette burns. A glass-fronted console attached to the wall above each scratched and pitted table allowed you to flip through a dozen panels and choose tunes by pushing buttons labelled with letters and numbers. The consoles had once been wired to a juke box, but the juke was gone, leaving orphaned songs like "A White Sports Coat and a Pink Carnation," "Blue Suede Shoes," and "Hand Jive."

The restaurant hummed with what Reena called the morning crowd—students from the college beside the park, stuffed with self-importance and thirsty for a caffeine fix, and regulars from the neighbourhood, sitting at the small tables and yakking or reading the paper while they sipped coffee and nibbled on muffins. Outside, the sun glinted off rush-hour windshields, and a streetcar rumbled and screeched to a stop at the traffic lights.

Behind me I heard the two-tone squeak of the swinging door to the kitchen. Reena slid into the booth across from me, an unfiltered cigarette in the corner of her mouth. She was wearing an almost-white apron, double-wrapped high above her waist, and a hairnet. I glanced at the "Absolutely No Smoking" sign above the console.

I still felt like she had cooked things up with my father to keep me away from home. But Reena didn't seem to care what anyone thought of her, including me, so she didn't play the role of the kindly, caring aunt. She hadn't tried to reform me. I had my room and a job in her restaurant, busing tables, sweeping up, lending a hand in the kitchen. She paid me, after deducting for "room and board." And she talked to me the same way she talked to everyone else, by showing respect and demanding it at the same time. It was understood that if I screwed up I would be gone.

We had reached that understanding one night about a week after Carpino dumped me at Reena's place. I had lain awake for hours after I climbed the stairs to my room, staring at the illuminated digits on the clock radio. A one, a zero, a colon, two more zeroes. And beside the little tail that hung off the upper left corner of the one, the tiny white letters, AM, with a red dot glowing next to them. I focused on those numbers for a long time, knowing they would never change.

I got out of bed and pulled on my clothes. I sneaked down the back stairs, threw on my coat, and closed the door carefully behind me. I ran across the deserted road and into the park, skirting the darkened buildings, heading for a stand of evergreens by the lake. I planned to stay there, more or less out of sight, until the trains started up early next morning, then head west toward Hamilton.

Maybe "planned" isn't the right word, because I hadn't worked out what I'd do when I got home—and I hadn't paid any attention to the weather. Gusts of freezing rain swept in from the lake, and within an hour my teeth were chattering, my hair was a helmet of ice, and every few seconds a shudder rattled my bones. Before long I found myself on the sidewalk beside the café, shoulders hunched against the cold, the side of my face burning from the sleet driven by the wind, banging on Reena's door. It took her a long time to answer.

"Forgot your key, I suppose," she said, standing in her nice warm vestibule wearing furry pink slippers, holding her woollen robe closed at her throat.

She knew damn well why I was standing out in the cold. "Yeah, right," I said.

"You look like a drowned cat."

"If you're planning to apply for the Mother of the Year award, I wouldn't bother," I said, pushing past her and clomping up the stairs.

But she made me come back down to the kitchen after I had changed my clothes, and she sat me down at the table.

"Look, Lee, even a fool knows when he's got no choices left."

"I guess you're right," I admitted.

"So, give this place a chance. It won't be so bad. If you want to call up your friends once in a while, I don't mind. Long distance to Hamilton isn't very expensive."

"Okay," I replied, suddenly tired. "I'm going to bed now."

I returned to the room upstairs, lay down in my clothes, and looked at the clock. I didn't tell her that I had no friends to call, anyway.

Now, sitting across from me in the booth, squinting against the smoke, she asked, "In the mood for a surprise?"

"I guess," I answered.

"Come on."

She led me through the kitchen and out the back door into the tiny courtyard, an area about the size of four cars parked side by side, enclosed by a two-metre-high brick wall. Huge flowerpots waited for the spring planting. Lawn furniture, rusting at the edges, had been shoved into one corner. Against the wall near the steel-clad door stood a bicycle.

"I've decided, if you agree, to start a delivery service," Reena said. "Solid, longtime customers only. And a few who aren't quite ready for Meals-On-Wheels but find home service convenient. Maybe a few deliveries a day."

"With that?" I said.

It was a hybrid, a cross between a street bike and mountain bike. The olive paint job was scaly and blotched with rust.

"Nobody," I said, "will want to steal *this* thing. It looks like a stripped-down tank."

"I don't know from bikes, but a friend told me it's in good condition. Said I could have it cheap."

I crouched and looked closer. Eighteen gears, no springs or shocks, wide tires with street treads, straight handlebars showing rust at the welds. A chain shiny with oil, new cables, clean hubs. A crappy-looking but well-maintained rig.

"Yeah, it's in good shape," I admitted. "I take it I'm the new delivery boy."

She pushed a strand of blonde hair off her forehead and grinned. "Let's say 'courier.' It sounds classier."

"How do you know I won't take off one day and never come back?"

"If you do, send back the bike. It cost me a hundred bucks. Anyway, what do you think?"

I was attracted by the idea of getting away from the boredom of the restaurant from time to time. And I liked the fact that Reena had said "if you agree."

"We'll need a good lock," I said. "And a rack. And pannier bags to carry the deliveries. Oh, and a map. I grew up in Hamilton, you know."

"Well," Reena said, flaming a new cigarette, "nobody's perfect."

FIVE

A COUPLE OF DAYS later, my first delivery took me to a home right on the lake at the bottom of 12th Street. The long, one-storey building looked more like a miniature factory than a house. Reena had warned me to be polite to the customers and had given me a long list of useless instructions. How hard can it be, I asked myself. Drop off the bag and leave. I didn't even have to handle the money—all the orders would be put on account.

Reena had said to take the food to the back door, so I coasted down the driveway into the yard, parked the tank against the house, and lifted the bag of food out of the pannier. There were whitecaps on the lake and a couple of Canada geese waddled across the lawn as if they owned the place. In the middle of the yard, a contraption shaped like an upended pail with a small box stuck on the side sat atop a pole. A little propeller turned slowly on the end of a rod that curved up and away from the main body.

I rapped on the door. A voice thundered from somewhere inside. "Yeah?"

"Reena's," I shouted, pushing the door open.

"Nope, this is Abe's." I heard a booming laugh. "Just kidding. Come through to the study. Dump the goodies on the kitchen table on your way by."

I went inside. A wide-shouldered man shouted a greeting—"Howya doing?"—from a chair where he sat tapping furiously on a computer keyboard. A spreadsheet filled the screen. On another monitor, coloured shapes jerked across a map of North America as if pulled by an invisible string. A large photo of a middle-aged woman had been placed between the computers. Cigar smoke hung in the air like a blue mist, and an empty glass stood on the desk beside a whiskey bottle and an ice bucket.

The man gave one last tap and slowly swivelled around to face me. His bald head was fringed with greying hair, and he wore a white shirt and dark tie under a paisley vest. A cigar jutted from the corner of his mouth, smoke curling from the long ash at the tip.

"Take a seat," he said, his voice like gravel.

I lifted a stack of printed sheets from the only other chair in the room and put them on the floor.

"Cuppa tea or coffee?" he offered.

"No, thanks. I'm okay."

"I'd offer you a drink, but you're driving," he chuckled as he reached for the bottle and poured a couple of inches of whiskey into the glass. Ice cubes clinked as he took a sip.

"So you're Reena's nephew," he said.

"Yup."

"I'm Abe Krantz. And you're—?"

"Lee."

"Reena's a *mensch*. She and my late wife were great friends. I was happy to hear she's starting a delivery service. Makes things easy for me. I don't like to cook much. I guess I'll be seeing you a few times a week. I don't get much company."

"I—"

"Central to Charlie three."

I looked up towards the source of the static and tinny voice. A small object the size of a desk phone, plastered with coloured buttons, sat on a shelf beside a row of reference books.

"It's a scanner," Krantz explained, picking up a remote. "Also a two-way shortwave radio." He pressed a button and a metallic computerized voice reeled off temperature and humidity, then started into a weather forecast. Krantz thumbed another button and the lights on the radio died. "Lets me listen in on the cops, fire department, ambulances and other stuff. Also the weather, including marine. I'm a watcher."

"A what?"

"Did you happen to notice my weather station in the yard?"

"Um . . ."

"That ungainly looking thing on the pole?"

"Oh. Yeah."

"It measures precipitation, temp, humidity, wind velocity and direction, and a few other things, then feeds the data to the receiver on the wall over there."

He pointed to a grey box with an LED screen full of numbers. "It's wireless. And it downloads to the computer every two hours. Also wirelessly. The computer compiles the data, develops local forecasts, charts patterns, et cetera, et cetera."

"Great," I said.

"So I always know what the weather will be tomorrow and forward."

"Why not just listen to the radio? I mean, the normal one."

"Because it isn't very accurate. Besides, this is more fun. There's lots more to it."

"I'll bet," I said, thinking, sounds pretty lame to me.

Krantz laughed. "We've barely met and I've already bored you to death with everything you didn't want to know about weather-watching. What do I owe you for the take-out?"

"Reena said she'd run a tab for you."

"Okay, well, let me give you something for dropping it off."

I got to my feet. "That's okay. Delivery's free."

He took out his wallet and handed me a five-dollar bill. "Maybe so, but take this anyway. As a favour to me."

I stuffed the bill into my pants pocket.

"Forgive me if I don't see you out," Krantz said. "Put the lock on the back door when you go, will you?"

"Sure. And thanks."

"See you soon," he said, and turned back to the keyboard. "And take your umbrella with you tomorrow. It's gonna rain."

I climbed onto the tank and wheeled out onto the street. Five bucks tip, I thought. This courier thing is okay.

———

That night, just after I climbed the stairs to my room, the phone rang in Reena's apartment. After she spoke for a few minutes, she called out, "Lee, it's for you."

The phone was in her kitchen. She was sitting at the little table by the window, a glass of wine beside the newspaper, a smoking cigarette in the ashtray beside it.

I picked up the phone. "Hello."

"Lee, it's Dad."

I hesitated for a moment, then, without saying anything, cut the connection. Reena looked up from her paper, her face neutral.

"See you in the morning," I said.

I trudged back upstairs and threw myself onto my bed, facing the wall. I knew he'd call back, maybe tomorrow, maybe in a few days. He'd keep at it. He was stubborn— "determined," he used to say to my mother. "Bullheaded," she'd reply with a smile.

I rolled over and kicked off my shoes, my eyes coming to rest on a plastic tumbler on my night table. I had brought it upstairs earlier in the evening, full of cola. I remembered the mornings when I was a little kid. When I got up and padded into the kitchen, cotton-headed with sleep and rubbing my eyes, my breakfast would be ready. My own special cereal bowl with my name printed in a line around the inside of the rim, *LeeLeeLee,* in one continuous word. My own white plastic tumbler with the red spaceship on the side in a cloud of blue stars, full of apple juice. A big silver spoon with CN engraved on the handle. A carton of cold milk and a box of puffed wheat—unsweetened because

Mom was always on a campaign against refined sugar. Mom sitting in her housecoat, reading the paper.

The morning after she was rushed to the hospital, my father had laid out my breakfast, and when I came into the kitchen and saw it, I freaked, knocking the milk carton onto the floor, flinging the cereal box across the room, sweeping the glass and bowl off the table, crying and screaming.

"What's the matter?" my father said over and over as I wailed. "What's the matter?" He finally figured out what I had been unable to explain. He had put out the wrong bowl, used the wrong glass, chosen the wrong spoon. He mopped up the lake of milk and puffed wheat, and made things right. I ate my breakfast, sniffling, not sure what had happened. From then on, the morning routine never changed.

But I guess I did. I stopped eating puffed wheat. Stopped breakfast altogether, even stopped gulping down the juice as I flew out the door, late for school. When I was in high school, right up to the day he kicked me out, I saw the same damn bowl and spoon and tumbler in the same damn place at the table every morning. Like he was making some kind of point. Like he was trying to preserve something we both knew was gone.

SIX

BEFORE I BEGAN THE day's assassination of soup vegetables, Reena handed me a paper bag and asked me to take it to Andrea, the pharmacist. I hung up my apron and perched my paper hat on the knife block.

The Lakeshore Pharmacy occupied the corner of Lakeshore Boulevard and 17th Street, a block east of the restaurant. I knocked at the back door off the alley that ran behind the buildings fronting Lakeshore Boulevard. Andrea Gauthier was a small, good-looking woman with brown eyes and long chestnut hair. She came into the café once in a while. I handed her the bag, warm and aromatic from the hot coffee and muffins inside.

"Thanks, Lee," she said, placing the package on a table surrounded by cartons and shelves packed with overstock.

"No sweat," I replied, turning to go.

"Um, Lee, do you have a minute?"

The door hissed shut. "Sure."

Andrea sat down and opened the bag, pried the lid off the coffee, and took a sip, letting out a contented sigh. She dug for a muffin. "Reena says you're doing take-out on wheels now."

"Yeah, just started last week."

"I was wondering, would you be interested in making the odd delivery for us? I'd clear it with Reena first, of course," she said around a mouthful of muffin when she saw me hesitate. "I could pay you up front each time. We have an account system for our regulars—you know, the shut-ins and so on, so you wouldn't have to keep track of any money. What do you say?"

I couldn't explain to her why I hesitated, could hardly put it into words for myself. I wasn't used to people relying on me. The other day Abe Krantz had invited me into his home, given me a tip, trusted me to leave and lock the door behind me. It's okay to be depended on, but it's also another chance to screw up.

Andrea had small, even teeth and full lips, and when she smiled the corners of her eyes turned up a fraction.

"Sure," I said. "Any time." I didn't tell her that I would have couriered for her for free.

"Well, how about this afternoon? I have a prescription for a guy over on 13th Street. He, er, doesn't get out much."

"One of the shut-ins?"

"More of a *stay*-in. He's a little, well, unusual. Say, about two?" she added, without elaborating.

"See you then," I said.

———

Bruce Cutter lived in a brick two-storey north of Morrison Street. I pushed the tank up the buckled sidewalk and dragged it onto the verandah. A waist-high metal box, with MAIL painted in white on a blue background, sat beside the door, a big padlock on the hasp. As I reached into the pannier for the pharmacy bag, I noticed that the drapes on the bow windows were closed. Little metal disks suspended on irregular lengths of black thread seemed to float behind the glass. I looked closer. The disks had been cut from the bottoms of cans.

Wondering what kind of eccentric lived in such a gloomy house, I thumbed the doorbell and waited, hefting the bag. This guy was either a hypochondriac or really sick, judging from the four fat pill containers inside. I pushed the button again. Andrea had said that Cutter hardly ever left the place. I tried knocking.

A hollow metallic voice commanded me to "Step back from the door."

I took a pace backward. A video camera, painted the same colour as the door trim, pointed its single eye at me. Beside it was a speaker grille.

"What do you want?" the voice demanded.

I held up the pharmacy bag. "Lakeshore Pharmacy," I said.

There was a long pause. "How do I know for sure?"

"Because I'm standing on your verandah with a bag full of pills that Andrea asked me to drop off. If you want, I'll just leave it here by the door."

"Enter." I heard a lock release.

I stepped into a dark vestibule, and the door closed behind me with a *thunk*. A little panel in the door before me slid aside for a moment, then slipped back in place. I heard a variety of metallic clunks and clicks—more locks being disengaged, I guessed—then the door opened slowly to reveal a tall, stooped man in an open bathrobe, wrinkled pajamas, and ratty slippers.

Cutter looked to be in his thirties. He was pale, unshaven, and gave off a sour odour. Coloured racing cars dashed around the legs of his pajamas.

I held out the bag, ready to leave quickly. But he wanted to shake hands. "Cutter," he announced solemnly.

His hand was cold. "Lee," I said.

He wiped his palm on his robe, as if I had contaminated him. "First or last?" he asked.

"Huh?"

"Lee. First name or last?"

"Oh, first. Lee Mercer. Drug squad," I added.

Cutter smiled. He had green eyes that burned with a strange fire, and freckles. The corner of his right eye twitched repeatedly. "Well, come on in."

Without taking his eyes off me, he backed into a large, dimly lit room. Shelves jammed tight with books covered the walls. Uneven stacks of files, magazines and books hid the tops of trestle tables. Three computers glowed from a long desk, flanked by printers, a scanner, other electronics, a stack of software manuals, and a chaos of CDs and DVDs. At one end of the desk, a cluster of small TV monitors perched on top of a bank of VCRs showed black-and-white images of locations outside the house. I recognized the tank leaning against the verandah railing. A row of filing cabinets lined a short hallway leading to a kitchen at the back.

There was something about the house, besides the stale air and musty odour, that made me feel kind of trapped. Then I realized what it was. There was no natural light.

"I'll take that," Cutter said, and I handed him the bag. He carried it through to the kitchen, tore it open, rummaged around for a moment, and came back with it.

"Tell Andrea I put the empties inside," he said.

There were four pill containers in the bag, along with lids. "I don't get it," I said.

"She's always after me to remember my meds," he said, his eye half-winking rapidly. "If I don't, I slide into Never-Never Land again. I start colouring outside the lines. Mixed metaphor. So I return the empties to prove I've been a good boy."

You could have dumped the pills down the toilet, too, I thought.

"I have to get back to work, now," Cutter said, pointing over his shoulder to the desk with his thumb.

I turned to go, nearly tripping on a stack of books that wobbled and then collapsed, spewing across the rug.

"Sorry," I muttered.

"My fault. I pile my library books by the door so I don't forget to take them back. A little trick to help my memory. The dope burns holes in it." He got to his knees and rebuilt the tower. "The library's only two blocks away, but I never seem to get over that way."

He looked up from where he was kneeling, in his bathrobe and pajamas, his eye flinching as if it had a mind of its own. He was like a kid, as if the world was too much for him.

"I guess I could drop them off for you," I said.

His eyes narrowed. He shook his head. "Oh, no, you—" He seemed to catch himself. "Well . . . okay, er, thanks."

He got to his feet and walked back to the kitchen, returning with a supermarket bag. He put the books inside, and handed them over. I stepped into the vestibule.

"Bye," he said abruptly, and slammed the door. I heard the mechanical clicks and thumps of the locks.

Before I mounted the tank, I took a look back at Cutter's house. Afternoon sun glinted off the shiny disks in the upstairs windows. I rode the two blocks to the library and hauled the books inside. The man behind the counter told me they were all overdue. I owed three dollars in fines.

"Perfect," I said.

Later that day I walked under a threatening sky to Lakeshore Pharmacy. I passed between aisles jammed with dental floss, hair colouring, condoms and cold remedies to the high counter at the back. Andrea stood with a phone clamped between shoulder and ear, talking and punching keys on a computer, while her assistant, a skinny guy in a spotless lab coat, pushed pills off the edge of a plastic tray into a trough with a little spatula, mumbling to himself.

I held up Cutter's bag and Andrea nodded. I waited 'til she got off the phone.

"Come on back, Lee," she said.

I rounded the end of the counter and followed her through a door leading to the store room where I had met her earlier. She took the bag and solemnly examined the containers.

"Thanks, Lee," she finally said. "Everything go all right?"

"Sure," I answered.

"Nothing, er, unusual?"

I smiled. "How am I supposed to answer that?"

Andrea laughed, her eyes crinkling. "Let's sit down," she said. "I could use a break. Been on my feet all morning."

I didn't mind spending time with Andrea. She was attractive and smart and spoke to me like an equal, even though she was a university-educated pharmacist and I was your average screw-up and dropout. Besides, I was curious about Cutter.

"Bruce is a sweetheart," she began. "Sometimes, when he comes in to fill his prescriptions, he wants to talk. He goes on and on as if he's trying to cram as many words into a moment as he can. But most of the time I can't get a word out of him. He has some . . . mental problems."

"I figured," I said.

"A number of years ago, Bruce told me, he came down with appendicitis—this was before he moved into the neighbourhood. He never said where he was from. Anyway, the attack was so bad he was rushed to the hospital and the doctors operated. Bruce swears that, while they had him unconscious, they implanted a microchip in his brain. Not long after he returned home he began to receive signals beamed from Buffalo. He saw people who weren't there and heard voices commanding him to do things he knew he shouldn't do."

I laughed. "Buffalo?"

Andrea frowned and looked displeased, then let out a giggle. "I know," she said, struggling to regain a serious face. "It's terrible, but funny at the same time. Anyway, he's under psychiatric care. Unless he takes his medication, he's delusional and paranoid. He goes right over the edge."

"Into Never-Never Land," I put in.

"Pardon?"

"That's how he described it to me."

Andrea shook her head. "It's such a shame. Bruce is brilliant. He's—was—a software designer. He invented a computer game while he was at university. When he told me that, I didn't believe him. You know. With all his other ramblings. But I looked up the game on the Net. He's the author, all right. It's still one of the most popular games on the market, even though it's totally nonviolent. It emphasizes intelligence and quick wits. Every time it goes into another edition, Bruce gets higher royalties. He's rich. Not that it does him any good. He has no family, no siblings, and his parents are dead. And he's—"

I finished her sentence. "—colouring outside the lines."

Andrea shrugged. "All over the page," she said.

SEVEN

HAMILTON BAY ELEMENTARY WAS close to our apartment, in a neighbourhood of grimy streets and factories, and bullies grew as tough there as the weeds that choked the cracks in the schoolyard pavement. Being small for my age, I was the perfect target.

Larry Wildfong was in grade eight, bigger than most, and mean. Somewhere along the line he had picked up the idea that he was clever. He and his crew hung around outside the schoolyard gate, blocking the sidewalk and forcing people to walk around them, smoking, hassling girls with dirty jokes or gestures. Every morning when I turned the corner onto Skene Street, a ball of fear in the pit of my stomach, I hoped that when I got to the gate they'd be preoccupied with someone else, or not in the mood to give me trouble that day.

There was nowhere to go for help. The teachers didn't have a clue what was going on under their noses, or didn't know what to do about it, or didn't care, which all amounted to the same thing. Besides, ratting on someone was something you just didn't do. When I had complained to my father, his solution was to "stand up to them." Exactly how I was supposed to stand up to four or five guys, all bigger and older than me and bursting with confidence, he didn't say.

One day not long after my mother's funeral, I plodded to school, sad and confused by her death. In a strange way, the hollowness she had left behind was a powerful presence that my father and I stepped around and didn't talk about. It was so strong and so real that it was almost physical, and it hurt, and it sapped away energy and eagerness, as if I was dragging an invisible weight behind me. That morning I was frightened because, since I had woken that morning, I couldn't remember her face.

When I thought of her I saw the funeral mask of a stranger, hair stiff and unnatural, skin tight and coated with powder, the not-asleep look of her closed eyes as she lay in her coffin. My mother had never used hairspray or make-up. I was terrified that, for the rest of my life, each time I thought of her I would see only the rigid face that wasn't the real her.

I heard the shouting even before I turned the corner. Wildfong and his gang were kicking a book back and forth like a deflated soccer ball while Sam Greenberg stood by, clutching his violin to his chest. I was relieved that they were preoccupied with Sam. Maybe I could slip by unnoticed. I walked faster, skirted the knot of bodies and flashing feet, and made for the gate.

"Hey! There's Mercer!" I heard. "Are you a Jew, too, Mercer?"

A couple of guys, their feet scuffling on the pavement, left the game and cut me off. As the rest sauntered over and formed a circle around me, Sam snatched up his book and sprinted toward the school, his violin case banging against his leg as he ran.

Larry pushed my chest. "Where do you think you're going, runt?"

I kept my eyes on the asphalt between my shoes, lips pressed together. I felt rather than heard someone move in behind me. A favourite trick of Wildfong's bunch was to have Larry hold your attention while another guy knelt behind you. Then, with a shove, Wildfong would send you toppling back onto your head.

I shuffled to the side, surprised that, for once, I wasn't scared. Each time the pack had come after me in the past, I had stood head down, unwilling to look Wildfong in the eye. I had waited with my heart pounding, the inside of my head echoing unmouthed words, please, please, let me go, leave me alone.

Now, the fear was absent. What could be greater than the dread I had carried with me since my father's shout had roused me from bed that morning?

"I'm talking to you, runt," Wildfong snarled.

And then something flared up inside me and, with my teeth clenched and my fists flying, I threw myself at him.

Caught by surprise, Wildfong stumbled backwards and fell, with me on top of him. My fists connected a few times before the pack hauled me off Larry and began to kick and punch me, cursing and grunting with the effort. I rolled to the side, scrabbled to my feet, and launched myself at

Wildfong again, hammering his chest a few times before he knocked me backwards with a punch to my face.

"Hold the little bastard," he hissed.

The others grabbed me from behind, pinning my arms. As Wildfong stepped forward I aimed a kick at his crotch, missed, caught him in the knee. With a boxer's combination, he slugged me in the face and stomach. The hands released me and I fell to my knees, gasping. Surrounded, I forced myself to stand, eyes on Wildfong.

By this time a small crowd had gathered, but they stayed back, watching. "Fight, fight!" someone shouted, but the others didn't take up the chant the way they normally would.

I hurled myself at Wildfong again, swinging, my fists catching only air. He sidestepped, throwing out a leg, and I sprawled face first on the ground, hands forward to catch my fall. Laughter from the crowd. I got up once more, turned to face him. I spat blood, wiped my hands on my jeans to clear away the grit embedded in my palms.

"Had enough, runt?" he said.

This time I landed one on his chin before he counter-punched and put me on the ground again. I got up, swung, missed, spun like a drunken dancer, and fell. A few more laughs from the onlookers, weaker this time. Once more I hauled myself up, stood wobbling, gathering what little strength I had left.

The guys in the pack began to sidle toward the school-yard gate, as if avoiding a vicious dog. No sneers on their faces, now. They looked almost embarrassed. "Stay down, you stupid prick," one of them said, "or he'll kill you." But Wildfong, unsure of what to do, moved with them, backing up across the schoolyard like a crayfish, muttering

"Quit it," pushing me away or tripping me every time I made another pathetic rush at him, until one last kick in the gut put me down for good. I looked up to see Larry and his pack disappear behind the doors of the school just as Mrs. Laurier came around a corner of the building.

Limping and bleeding, I made my way back home. Once inside the apartment, I tossed my clothes into the laundry and took a hot bath, sitting in the steam, working out a story to tell my father when he got home. Later, I explained that a bunch of guys I didn't know had jumped me in the park near our apartment. He bought the lie, shaking his head and muttering as he examined my battered face, his eyes brimming with sadness, as if the beating had been his fault. I stood quietly, holding back my anger that he hadn't been there to help me, that he was never there.

That wasn't my last fight, but no one bullied me again. Without planning it or even knowing what I had been doing, I had learned my lesson. You had to stand up to them. To everyone. No matter what the odds, never show weakness, always be willing to take them on, never give in. They had to know that it would cost them something, even if they won.

EIGHT

You didn't have to know anything about the restaurant business to see that Reena was never going to make a lot of money. She opened three times a day, with periods in between when the doors were locked. The morning shift offered coffee, muffins and toast and donuts, fried egg sandwiches and omelettes. Lunch meant salad, soup of the day, and a variety of sandwiches. Dinner was a choice between the two dishes that Reena decided to cook that day. The menus were chalked on a blackboard above the coffee counter.

She made a huge pot of soup in the morning, using vegetables that I chopped up and whatever meat was left over from the day before, adding spices that she shook out of jars without labels. She made the sandwiches to order, standing at the wood block in the kitchen, her hands a blur, a cigarette dangling from the corner of her mouth. If the customers noticed the odd hint of ash in their food, they never complained.

She and I ate our meals in the kitchen, except at night, when she sometimes invited me down to her apartment for a snack.

Reena didn't talk much about herself. I barely remembered her from my childhood—just the one extended visit when I was little and my mom was still alive. My father never mentioned her until the day he packed me off to live with her like a bundle of used clothes you'd ship to a charity. And she didn't pelt me with questions about myself. Maybe my father filled her in on what a failure and lost cause I was, maybe not. She didn't seem to care.

Which was just fine with me. If I had to admit it, I'd say I didn't mind living with her at all. I liked her. As long as I did my work, she left me alone. I didn't have to go to school or answer to anybody. I liked the fact that I was earning my keep, even a little extra. I was saving up to buy a used TV for my room. True, I had an axe hanging over my head—Sergeant Carpino's threats—but I decided to let that go for a while. All that had happened back home. There was nothing back there for me, anyway.

I was emptying the dishwasher, my face bathed in steam, while Reena cut chunks of beef—the dinner menu, she announced, was beef stew or nothing, she was too tired to put two choices on the menu that day—when the phone rang.

"I'll get it," she said, wiping her hands on her apron. Behind me I heard, "Hello. Oh, hi, Doug. Yeah, he's right here."

I shook my head, mouthed No, and lifted a stack of hot plates to the shelf.

Reena held her hand over the mouthpiece. "At least say hello to him," she said. "He—"

I headed for the door. "Come on, Lee," she insisted. "Do me a favour."

Muttering to myself, I took the phone from her.

"Hello."

"Hi, Lee. How's it going?"

His voice was friendly, casual, but forced. In the background I heard the whine of a pneumatic wheel gun, the hiss of a hoist, a clang.

"All right."

"Reena tells me you're doing real good at the café."

"I guess."

"That's great. Glad to hear it."

Silence. Reena rolled her eyes, waved her hand as if to say, I give up.

"Things are working out okay, then."

What did he want me to say? Yes, father, you can put your guilt back on the shelf? You threw me out but it's the best thing you could have done for me because now I'm happy and content and life is wonderful?

"I'm fine," I said.

"That's good, so—"

"Not that you give a shit."

There was another, longer pause.

"Well," he said, his voice flat, "I guess I better get back to work. I'm in the middle of a tune-up."

"Don't let me keep you."

He hung up without saying goodbye.

———

She was one of the regulars—meaning she turned up a few mornings a week, sat in one of the booths with a coffee, and nibbled at a fried egg sandwich while she busied herself on her laptop. I figured her for a student at the high school up at 18th and Birmingham, or maybe the college. She had shoulder-length black hair with a tight wave in it, light brown skin, and dark eyes.

The first day I saw her, I went to bus her table, even though all she had was a plate and cup. I plunked down my plastic tub and picked up her plate. "Another coffee?" I asked.

She looked up from the screen and gave me a wide smile. "No, thanks," she said. "Better not. You the boss?" she asked playfully.

"No. I'm the hired help."

"You don't even rate a name tag?"

It took me a second to catch on. "Lee," I said.

"Well, Lee," she said, draining her cup and placing it inside the tub. "Don't forget this."

I stepped back as she wriggled to the edge of the booth and stood up. She was my height, well built, and she smelled lemony. She closed the laptop and shoved it into her backpack.

"See you," she said, shouldering the pack, and she was out the door before I could get her name.

So the next time I saw her, on a rainy morning a few days later, I worked my way toward her booth, collecting cups and plates and cutlery, wiping down the tables. She had finished her sandwich, but the coffee stood beside her notebook, three-quarters full, a skim of cream on top. She was wearing a tight pink sweater and black denims, and in profile she was enough to stop the breath in my throat.

"How's it going?" I said, taking her plate.

"Not," she said, reversing her pencil and erasing some numbers from the page. "Know anything about periodic tables?"

"The only tables I'm familiar with are usually covered with dirty dishes."

She laughed, sat back, and tossed the pencil down.

"It's not fair, you know," I said.

"What's not fair?"

"You know my name . . ."

"Eileen," she offered.

We made small talk for a few minutes while the traffic hissed by on the street outside, the café door opened and closed as customers came and went, the tinkle of spoons and soft rumble of talk around us. I could have gone on like that for hours. Eventually, she looked at her watch and packed up her stuff and left, leaving the fragrance of her citrus cologne behind her.

It went like that for a couple of weeks, and then one Friday she came in earlier than usual, as if in a hurry, and got herself a coffee without ordering anything to eat. While she tapped away at her keyboard, she kept looking toward the door. I hung back. I had decided to ask her to go out with me and I was working up the courage. There wasn't much chance, I figured—her a serious student, me a dropout living above a café with my aunt—but I was going to give it a try.

I was taking a break at my booth, waiting for my chance, when a stranger came in. A tall, college type—designer backpack, leather jacket, expensive trainers. Probably had a flashy sports car parked in the college lot. He marched straight to Eileen's booth, planted his feet, and began to talk. I couldn't make out what he was saying but his body language was loud and aggressive.

She said something and he grabbed her arm. She shook him off, and this time I heard her tell him "No!"

He clutched her arm again, with two hands this time, as if he meant to drag her out of the booth. I scrambled out of my seat.

"Let her go!" I said.

He turned to me, his face reddened. "Mind your own frig—"

I drilled him in the rib cage, felt my knuckles connect with bone. He grunted in pain, dropping Eileen's arm, and I shoved him back. His eyes signalled what he would do, and before he had the chance, I stepped closer and threw two solid punches into his face before he hit the floor. He groaned and rolled over, struggling to his hands and knees.

"Stop! Stop!" I heard behind me, but the words didn't register. Fists pummelled my shoulders. Somebody was screaming.

"Get up," I hissed, ready to give him more.

Someone was still pounding away at me. I swirled to face him. It was Eileen, her face livid, her teeth clenched. Why was she hitting *me*? I grabbed her wrists. "Calm down," I told her, as she yanked free of my hold. "It's all right—"

"What? You're going to beat *me* up now?" she yelled.

I became aware of faces at the tables, staring at me as if I was in a cage.

Eileen's eyes flared, her fists clenched. "What's the matter with you?" she shouted. "You could have hurt him."

"But—"

"You think I needed you to save me, is that it, hero? Christ, you're as bad as him!"

"I—"

She quickly gathered her things, helped the guy to his feet and, after glaring in my direction, helped him out the door.

Reena was not pleased. Later that morning, after she had hung the CLOSED sign in the window, she sat me down in the kitchen. "I'm trying to run a business here," she began.

"He was going to hit her," I said, cutting her off. "I had to do something."

"Whether you had to do something or not isn't the issue," Reena said, tucking her hair behind one ear. She shook a cigarette free of the pack, plucked it out with her lips, and lit up. "What's important is how you handled the problem—assuming you had to do anything at all."

"What else could I have done?"

"Use your imagination," she said. "But keep in mind what I just said. I don't run a couples' counselling service. You tell people like them to take their problem somewhere else. That's it."

"Guys like that need a lesson."

"Lee, think about it. You hit him so he wouldn't hit her. What's wrong with the picture?"

"What do you mean?" I asked.

Reena stubbed out her cigarette on the saucer she was using as an ashtray and stood up.

"I got some work to do," she said.

There were things I couldn't say to Reena. About the darkness that gushed into my brain like water from a broken pipe. About the compulsion in my muscles, the voice that screamed in my ear to hit and hit and pile up hurt, to keep going until whoever was on the receiving end had collapsed to helplessness. I couldn't tell her that I knew exactly what she meant. Knew she was right.

Before I got kicked out of school the second time, I had a girlfriend the kids had nicknamed Barbie—her real name was Beth—because she was slender and had long blonde hair framing a pretty face. All the girls envied her and all the guys wanted her. Maybe girlfriend is the wrong word. Maybe it was all in my mind.

We went to the movies one Saturday night, necked through the whole picture. Afterwards, I had it bad. I saw only her. Heard only her. Wanted to escort her to school in the morning, to walk her home at the end of the day. I engineered things so I met her between classes. I called her every night.

We went out a few more times. I began to think she was mine. Thought she wanted it that way. Then one day when I went to meet her after school at our usual place—outside the main office—she didn't turn up. I asked one of her friends if she had seen Beth.

"Before or after she got into Freddie Tanner's Audi?" she sneered.

On the phone that night, Beth's mother told me Beth couldn't come to the phone. She had too much homework.

A few days later, I was waiting in the library parking lot across from her house when Tanner dropped her off. I saw his profile through the side window, hair swept back off his forehead, a big ring on his finger, before he peeled away.

I called out to her. She didn't look happy to see me, but she acted cool, as if it was her brother she'd been out with. She walked across the road and sat on a bench off to the side, away from the library door.

I stood in front of her, hemming her in, and demanded to know why she'd been ignoring me. A toxic brew churned in my guts—humiliation, anger, frustration.

"I just didn't feel like being with you lately," she said, as if that explained everything.

"What are you talking about? I don't get it."

"Look, Lee, no offense, but sometimes you're like . . . like a blanket."

I felt the tingle in my limbs that sometimes came before the black rush. "What the hell are you talking about?"

"You're suffocating me. Every time I turn around, you're there. I need room to breathe."

"I thought we were—"

"We were what? We went out a few times. I like you."

"Then why were you with him?"

"Because he's fun, that's why. And he doesn't hover over me like a demented guardian angel."

"You're nothing but a tramp," I blurted.

Her eyes narrowed. "Don't you dare call me names, you pathetic loser!"

I slapped her so hard her head snapped back. Eyes wide with shock, she jumped to her feet, her hand on her reddening cheek.

I tried to put my arms around her. "Beth, Beth, I'm sorry. I didn't mean—"

She struggled free. "Don't touch me! Don't come near me!" She ran into the street. A car skidded to a stop, tires yelping and horn blasting. The driver leaned out. "Watch where you're going, you stupid—"

But she was gone up her front sidewalk and into the house.

I stood in the parking lot, shaking, as the darkness ranted in my veins.

NINE

My second delivery to Cutter's was similar to the first—like entering a bank vault. He was polite but, after handing over his empties, got rid of me as fast as he could, slamming the door behind me. My third delivery—this time bringing aspirins, antacid, and dental floss rather than the meds—he greeted me in a V-neck sweater, cords and loafers. He was clean-shaven and his hair was combed, although he was still as pale as milk. He invited me in and almost smiled.

He handed me a key. "Mind picking up my mail for me?"

I returned to the verandah and opened the metal box, retrieving a bunch of envelopes and one package. Cutter locked the doors behind me, raked his hair with his fingers. "Did you make sure to secure the mailbox?"

I nodded. He took the mail and dumped some of it onto an already overburdened table. The rest he fed into a huge shredder under the table, ignoring the cascade of paper ribbons spilling from its maw.

"Excuse me for a second," he said, and went to his desk. "I'm just printing off the morning's gleanings." He punched a button. A printer began to crank out pages.

"The morning's what?" I asked.

Cutter jumped up and snapped his fingers. "A seat," he said to the ceiling, then scooted into the kitchen. He rushed back with a wooden chair and set it down by the desk.

"It's part of my inquiries," he began, looking at a spot over my right shoulder. "I scan certain newspapers and research services on the Net every day." He held up a finger, as if delivering a lecture. "If you ever use the Net remember that they can track every move you make, plus read all your e-mail, plus invade your computer, spy on all your files, and leave cookies behind. You've got to stay sharp. Using the Net is like sitting naked in a glass house. Where was I? Oh, right. I also read certain magazines. You have to be careful, 'cause most mags are just propaganda sheets for them." He pointed to a large-screen TV in a cabinet, the doors hanging open. I hadn't noticed it before. "Got three dishes on the roof, all technically illegal. I'm tuned in to everything. It's the only way I can keep track of them."

"Them?"

"Yeah."

"Who's Them?"

"You mean you don't know?"

"I don't get out much," I replied.

Cutter smiled. His eye began to twitch. "You're making fun of me."

"No, really, I'm not," I said. Which was true. "It's just that, well, I have no idea what you're talking about."

He searched my face, as if reading a map. "Okay, I believe you. I'm not very clear sometimes, am I?" In an instant, he was on his feet. "Want some tea?"

"Um, sure."

A few minutes later we were sitting again, this time in his kitchen. There was one large window that probably looked out onto the back yard, but it was covered with thick curtains. I would have bet that there were aluminum disks hanging between the curtains and the glass. The window in the back door, which was locked with deadbolts, was also covered.

The countertop and sink were piled high with used dishes that gave the room an overripe odour. Cutter had poured tea for both of us and seemed to have forgotten his already. I sipped mine—black. He hadn't offered milk or sugar.

"Take today's research," he said, picking up where he had left off. "I'm tracking down the financial statements of the corps"—corporations, he explained when I tried to interrupt—"that profit from sweatshop labour in the athletic clothing industry. They subcontract the manufacturing to jobbers in the third world—China, the Philippines, Mexico, Vietnam, lots of places where people are starving and will work for next to nothing—and the jobbers in turn subcontract to others who run the sweatshops. That way, the big corps in Europe and North America that sponsor tennis matches and basketball players and golf tournaments can pretend they're not accountable for what goes on in the sweatshops. If you go up to the mall on the

Queensway you can find a half-dozen stores that sell their stuff. A shirt that costs twenty-three bucks—guess how much they pay the girl who sewed it together."

"Don't have a clue."

"Eight cents."

"Eight *cents*?"

"There are twenty-two separate operations to produce the shirt. Five to cut the material, six to attach labels—like that. The process is all broken down right to the second. Literally. The factory produces a shirt every six point six minutes. Know what that means?"

I played along. "What?"

"The pressure on the assembly line is enormous. A worker performs the same miniscule operation about two thousand times a day, sitting at her machine twelve to fourteen hours at a stretch."

Eyes alight, spit flying, Cutter tumbled on with more of the same, his words gushing out of his mouth as if his speaking apparatus couldn't keep up with his brain. Then he stopped.

"More tea?"

I drained my mug. "No, thanks."

"Sorry to ramble on," he said, rubbing his hands together.

Ramble was definitely not the word for Cutter's headlong torrent of words. He looked around as if he'd just realized he was in the kitchen. "I gotta get this mess cleaned up."

"That's what the dishwasher is for," I said.

Cutter eyed the appliance as if it had magically appeared only seconds before and said sheepishly, "Forgot how to use it."

I stood up. I doubted that the guy who manipulated all the electronics in the other room couldn't use a dishwasher, but I also doubted he was focused enough to manage it. His mind was on his research.

"Okay," I said. "I can load it up and get it going, I guess. Done it a million times at Reena's."

"Great!" he said. "They fire them if they get pregnant."

"The dishes?"

"No, the girls. In the sweatshops."

Cutter dashed into his office as if he had forgotten something. I heard him at the keyboard as I stacked the dishwasher and turned it on. While it sloshed and groaned, I filled the sink with soapy water and finished off the overflow, setting the pots and dishes and cutlery in a rack to dry. I wiped down the counter and hung the rag over the faucet. I would never admit it to anyone, especially Reena, but I didn't mind washing dishes. It was satisfying, in a way.

In the other room I found Cutter standing with a handful of letters.

"Could you drop these at the post office on 9th for me, Lee? Don't put them in a street box. They're too easy to break into."

"How come you don't trust the post boxes but you trust me?"

Cutter inspected my face again, as if trying to memorize every hair and pimple. "Good question," he said. His gaze slid off my face and wandered the room. "I can't explain it. I just feel like you wouldn't let me down." He seemed to focus again, and handed me a twenty-dollar bill. "I sure appreciate this, Lee."

I counted the envelopes, taking a quick look at the destinations. Various government offices, two for the United Nations, one for the Prime Minister. "Twenty is way too much, Cutter. A ten ought to cover it."

"Keep the change. A tip."

"No, give me a ten." I figured ten bucks would pay for the mail and the library fine he had stuck me with.

He rummaged around in a drawer filled with bills and coins and gave me the money.

"Did you know you forgot to put your return address on these?" I asked.

Cutter smiled crookedly, his eye twitching. "They know who I am," he said. "They know all about me."

"And one more thing," I added, pulling open the vestibule door. "Those disks hanging in your windows. What are they for?"

Cutter cocked his head, as if I had asked the stupidest question in the world. "They deflect radio waves," he said.

TEN

I WAS RELAXING IN my booth, taking a break and letting my thoughts wander while the breakfast crowd got their caffeine and sugar fixes. Around me, the tinkle of spoons on saucers and cups, the grumble of conversation, the rustle of newspapers. The tables along the opposite wall were full, and everyone was reading the news. At one point, as if they had rehearsed it, almost all of them held their newspapers open at the same time, making a sort of billboard, each black-and-white patch floating between a pair of hands. A headline shouted that someone whose name I couldn't pronounce was on trial for war crimes in a city I had never heard of. A picture showed a man in a suit standing behind a podium, with a big sloppy grin on his face. Underneath, it said, GABLER ANNOUNCES ENVIRONMENTAL INITIATIVE. There was a story about the Sudan and Africa. An airline had gone bankrupt. And then, as people turned a page or shifted in their seats, the billboard broke up.

I pushed my half-eaten muffin away. I had never heard of Gabler or the man on trial, didn't know what the Sudan was, knew nothing about Africa or the airline. I couldn't have felt more empty-headed if the readers of the morning papers had stood by my table and peppered me with questions. And suddenly I was ambushed by a familiar image— me, on the outside of a building, looking through a locked window into a comfortable room. People relaxing around an open fire, laughing and talking together, people who understood how the world worked.

I was sick and tired of not knowing things. I shifted my eyes to the two guys by the café door, elbows on the table, heads together, the bills of their caps almost touching, then the students packed into the booth beside mine, arguing energetically about some book they were studying. Naturally, I hadn't read the book. Naturally, I hadn't even heard of it.

In high school, as far as I went, I got through my courses without much effort, collecting credits the way you'd pick up stale food you really didn't want in the cafeteria. But at the same time, although I never admitted it to myself, I always felt I was missing something. I knew I wasn't stupid.

I was ignorant.

Not exactly a cheery conclusion to come to. Not exactly a morale booster. But I had to admit it was true.

Why today? What had brought this on, the way you realize you've got frostbite only when your flesh begins to sting? Was it being around Cutter the brain so much, with his books and computers and far-out theories? Or Andrea, running her own business? Or Abe, with his weather maps and charts and storm-tracking software? Was it because Cutter was persuaded his work was important and Abe was having so much fun?

The next time I took Cutter's books back to the library—not overdue this time—and handed them in at the returns desk, I stood looking around at the ranks of shelves, the row of computers, the magazine rack. In grade nine we had had a library orientation class to teach us how the place operated and how to find stuff, but as usual I hadn't paid much attention. I didn't know what I wanted anyway. I was hopeless.

I turned to go. Behind me, I heard, "Can I help you find something?"

The guy on the other side of the desk looked more like a janitor than a librarian—rumpled jeans, baggy sweatshirt, a screwdriver in one hand, a stapler in the other. A pen hung from a cord around his neck. The cord was caught on a name tag that said CLANCY.

"Um, well, I was sort of looking for—" what? I had no idea. "A good book," I said stupidly.

Clancy looked me up and down. He figures I'm a bonehead, I thought.

"Why not try our Perennial Favourites table?" he said, pointing across the room with the screwdriver. "Over there. Call me if you need help." He went back to trying to unjam the stapler.

Wondering what "perennial" meant, I took a look at the display, just so Clancy wouldn't think I was a complete idiot. About two dozen books had been placed on wire racks so their covers were easily visible. I picked a few up, riffled the pages, put them back. Then I spotted a really thin one. *The Old Man and the Sea* it was called. A kiddie book. I flipped it open to the first page. *He was an old man who fished alone in a skiff on the Gulf Stream and he had gone eighty-four days now without taking a fish.* Didn't sound like a kid's story.

I checked the book out, took it back to my room, and tossed it onto the table beside my bed. Maybe I'd read it, maybe I'd just hold onto it for a while and return it to the library. Later that afternoon, I was in Andrea's drugstore to pick up a delivery to Mrs. Waslynchuck, a pensioner who lived alone—unless you counted the four cats—in an apartment on 33rd Street. In a rack of magazines and cross-word puzzle books I saw a paperback, *Increase Your Word Power! Add one word per day to your vocabulary! That's 365 new, useful words each year!* the cover said. Well, they can count, anyway, I thought, bending to replace the book. Then I changed my mind.

"I'd like to buy this," I told Andrea as I stuffed the little bag of Mrs. Waslynchuck's pills into my pannier.

"No way," she replied.

"Huh?"

"On the house," Andrea said, smiling. "Enjoy."

"Looks like we have a new customer," Reena said as I pushed through the door into the café kitchen. She was adding up the lunch receipts at a little table in the corner, a half-eaten sandwich and a glass of milk beside her calculator. "Andrea recommended him to us. He lives on 13th. Bruce something."

"Cutter?" I said. "He's ordering take-out?"

She tilted her head toward a brown bag on the counter under the phone. The top was folded over and the bill stapled to it. "Cold chicken sandwich and a tub of salad. An older fella, is he?"

"Thirties, maybe. In there somewhere."

"Sounded a little strange on the phone."

"Yup, that's Cutter all right," I replied, picking up the bag and heading for the back door.

Garbage bins and recycling boxes overflowing with cans and bottles stood like sentries along the curb on 13th Street. Pickup day. As I walked up Cutter's sidewalk, pushing the tank, the curtain at the front window twitched. I rang the bell, stepped back and made a face at the camera.

"Come on in, Lee."

Locks clicked and clacked. Cutter held the vestibule door open for me. "How are you?" he said pleasantly.

He led the way back to the kitchen. "Got time for a cup of tea?" he asked. "It's all ready." Cups, milk and sugar, and a teapot had been set out.

"I guess so."

"Help yourself. Have you eaten?"

"Yeah." I filled the mugs with coal-black tea. I wondered how long it had been brewing.

"Mind if I go ahead?" he asked, ripping open the bag. "I'm starved. I don't always have a very good appetite."

"No problem," I said, and sipped my tea. It was strong enough to dissolve the enamel off my teeth.

Cutter seemed calm. His hair was combed, and he was wearing khakis and a cardigan over a white shirt. As if he was going to class. Not that I'd know how university students dressed. He ate slowly, forking the salad directly from the plastic container, taking small bites from the sandwich. His eye wasn't twitching today.

Then he jumped up and scooted through to the office. I craned my neck to see what he was up to. He was bent over, holding the drape back a little, peering out the front window as if he didn't want to be seen. He stood up and returned to his chair and took a bite from the sandwich.

"What's up?" I asked.

"Oh, just checking, just checking." I waited. "The garbage," he said.

"Oh."

"Well, you know. Making sure no one is messing with it. Taking it."

"You're worried someone will take your garbage?"

"Yeah."

This is going to be one of those Cutter conversations where we skate around in circles, I thought, holding back a laugh. I didn't know whether I should humour him and keep talking, or let it go. But *not* talking would insult him, in a way. As if I thought he was a child and his conversation worthless.

"Isn't that why you put it out? To be trucked away?"

"No. Yes. I mean, take as in rob."

"Who would steal garbage?"

"They can find out everything about you by examining what comes out the back door," he explained. "That's why I use that big machine in the office. But even shredded paper can be reconstructed, I suppose."

It was hard to imagine a ring of trash thieves terrorizing the neighbourhood, but he was right, in a way. In the movies, cops and spies often scrounged through trash for information.

"They look for records, right?" I said. "Phone bills, credit card statements, and stuff."

"Right," Cutter replied, his face brightening. "You can construct a very reliable profile of a household by analyzing what they throw away. Our garbage is a mirror of our lives. Only with mayonnaise or peanut butter smears on it." He smiled, pleased at his joke.

"On the other hand, They already know everything about us. We live in an electronic wonderland. Most people have at least two bank credit cards, plus ones for gasoline, department stores, and so on. They don't realize it, but all those corps exchange information about their clients. A lot of them sell the information to marketing companies. That's where targeted junk mail comes from. There's no such thing as privacy."

If Cutter was aware that he was contradicting himself, he didn't show it. If he was right, why would anyone need to go through his garbage? But the more I was with him, the more I saw that being consistent wasn't part of the way his mind worked.

He popped the last bit of sandwich in his mouth and scrunched up the bag. "Feel like a walk?"

"You mean outside?"

"Of course. Just let me get my jacket."

I didn't mind going. It was entertaining, listening to his way-out theories, probably because they had a certain amount of truth to them—or sounded as if they did.

On the verandah, Cutter looked around, then plucked a hair from his head. He licked his fingers, ran the hair through the spit, and pressed it across the crack between the door and the frame.

"If anybody sneaks in while we're gone—"

"You'll be able to tell."

"Exactly."

I didn't mention the back door.

On the way down the street, Cutter's eyes darted from side to side. Every few steps he looked over his shoulder. Then he stopped as if he'd forgotten something.

"I've got to quit doing this," he said, and started walking again.

I wondered if he'd wanted to take a stroll because he was planning to tell me more conspiracies and he figured his house was bugged. I shook my head. You're getting paranoid, too, I told myself. Cut it out.

Around the corner of 13th and Lakeshore Drive, we passed through a gate in the high chain-link fence and entered the park. The lake was calm and slate-grey, the sky clear, the air chilly. To the west, the stacks of the Lakeview power generating station stood out against the sky. We walked along the bike path, stepping aside for roller-bladers and people pushing strollers.

"This whole park," Cutter said, ambling along, his shoulders hunched, his hands jammed into his pockets, "used to be a hospital for the mentally infirm. I read up on it after I moved here. It was actually a farm, and the inmates, the ones not locked down, grew vegetables and fruit. The idea was for the institution to be as self-sustaining as possible so it didn't put too much burden on taxpayers. And experts in those days thought hard work was good for the patients. A lot of them were mentally retarded—the patients, that is. Then attitudes changed and drugs came along—a mixed blessing, believe me. Most of the inmates were released to other facilities, or onto the street."

I thought of the Queen of Sweden and a few of the other astronauts who sat in the café in the mornings.

"The psychiatric hospital shut down," Cutter went on. "For a few years the buildings and grounds were rented out to movie companies and TV shows. Then the college took over most of the buildings and fixed them up."

He stopped and looked around. "I like to visit sometimes and sort of commune with the ghosts of the crazy people who used to live here."

He didn't say it, but I figured he was thinking that at one time he would have been one of the inmates, locked in a room behind bars, listening to the screamers as he tried to sleep.

"It's not much fun being crazy," he said, kicking a stone on the path.

I couldn't think of anything to reply to that, so we walked in silence. I was feeling a little guilty, coming along because I thought Cutter might say something funny—to me, not to him.

"You're a big help to me, Lee," he said after a while. Which made me feel more guilty.

"Me? How? All I do is bring you your prescriptions and stuff."

"You just are."

ELEVEN

As SPRING DRAGGED INTO summer, the café customers traded their sweaters and jackets for T-shirts and
shorts and skirts. Reena got the air conditioner serviced,
added caesar and chef's salads to the menu, and featured a
fruit plate at lunch time. The chalkboard menu didn't mention that all the pears and cherries and grapefruit segments
came out of cans. The college crowd thinned out when
classes ended and summer courses began. I never saw
Eileen again.

One sunny morning, I was tucked into my booth com-
posing sentences and writing them in my notebook, crossing out the ones that sounded wrong. "Ensconced" was my
word for the day, and I was having trouble using it in ways
that didn't sound stupid.

With my pen I drew a circle around the first "e" of
ensconced and coloured in the "o."

"You're outta cream," I heard from someone beside my booth. Someone who hadn't washed in a long while.

I looked up. "The Queen of Sweden was ensconced beside my booth," I wrote, then scribbled it out and threw down my pen.

"Morning, Your Majesty," I sighed.

"Never mind that, you're outta cream," she said.

I went into the kitchen, where Reena was flipping eggs on the grill, and took a jug of milk from the fridge and carried it to the coffee bar.

"There you go," I said to the Queen.

She nodded, her greasy grey hair falling across her face. She tossed the loose end of her blue and gold scarf over her shoulder—no warm weather clothes for her—and went about preparing her coffee. "Bad mood today?" she asked.

I returned to the booth and wrote, "The Queen's milk was ensconced in the café fridge." Satisfied, I closed the notebook and picked up my mug of Colombian.

The night before, Reena had called me down from my room on the third floor just as I was about to hit the sack. She was sitting in her easy chair, smoking, her glass of red on the chair arm, the evening news flickering on the muted TV. Her feet, clad in oversized fuzzy pink slippers, rested on a hassock.

"I need to have a talk with you," she had said, smoke streaming from her nostrils.

Dread blossomed in my chest. I stood in her doorway, one hand on the jamb. She's going to kick me out, I thought, anger seeping into my mind. She's had enough of me. That fight in the café a few weeks ago did it. Well, it wasn't as if I didn't deserve it, but leaving would be hard. More than I realized, I liked living with her. True, I had nothing to go "home" to, but it was more than that. I had thought she liked me.

"I guess I'm going back to my old man's," I said bitterly.

Reena looked at me over the rim of her wine glass. Her brow creased. "What makes you say that?'

"That's why you called me down here, isn't it?"

"You're way off base, Lee," she said. "Sit down and relax. Jesus, you're always so wound up."

I lowered myself to the edge of the bed. "Okay, what?"

"I spoke to your dad last night."

Here it comes, I thought.

"And, well, I have to tell you, he feels real bad about you not wanting to talk to him."

She paused, and I said nothing.

"But that's another story. Anyhow, he's agreed if you agree. I'd like you to stay on here for as long as you want. You're a big help to me, running the café. You're not the cheeriest angel in the choir. And," she smiled, "you can be a pain in the ass sometimes, but you work hard, and I like having you around. So, what do you say?"

I swallowed. My mouth was so dry I could hardly get my tongue to move. "Okay," I managed.

"Don't knock me over with your enthusiasm."

"No, really, I want to."

"Good."

I climbed the stairs to my room, shaking with relief, sat on my bed and looked around, and for the first time thought of it as just that—my room.

So the Queen had been dead wrong when she asked if I was in a foul mood. Just as she shuffled past the booth on her way to the door, my cell phone began to describe a lazy circle on the table. I picked it up.

"Yeah."

"There's a severe thunderstorm watch out for today. Keep your eye on the western sky from about three o'clock on."

"Hi, Abe."

"Howya this morning, Lee?"

"Good."

"Listen, you interested in another client? My lawyer— she's up on 8th Street in the old town hall building—she'd like to have you do the odd delivery for her."

"Okay," I said.

"Great. I'll give her your number, if that's all right."

"Sure, Abe."

"Drop by today, if you get a chance, willya? I got some paperwork to send up to Lakshmi—that's the lawyer."

Abe was a bookkeeper for a few small businesses on the Lakeshore. He also did tax returns for some of his neighbours.

"You can meet her then. Catch up with you later. Don't forget your raincoat." He broke the connection.

Cutter had bought me the phone a couple of weeks before, and he paid the fees. "I need to know I can get in touch with you whenever," he had told me. I asked if he minded if I used the phone for other deliveries. Could I give the number to Abe, Andrea, and Reena?

"No problem, good idea," he had replied. "But always remember, your calls are easy to monitor. They have microwave dishes all over town, hunting down signals. Keep your calls short and don't give too much away. Be vague. That throws Them off."

I saw Cutter three or four times a week now. I guess I worked for him, although it wasn't like that. I took his mail to the post office, delivered meals from the café, cleaned up his kitchen, brought him his pills and took the empties to Andrea, picked up books at the library and returned them when he was finished with them. I wasn't allowed to touch anything in his office, though, and I was absolutely forbidden to go upstairs.

We talked a lot, too. Cutter was lonely. And he was an interesting guy—hard to follow sometimes, but if I paid close attention to what he was saying, most of it made sense, eventually. Sometimes I told him about what I was reading. I had made my way through *The Old Man and the Sea*—it wasn't really about fishing—and Clancy had gotten me onto some other Hemingways.

One minute I felt sorry for Cutter, another, I admired him. He was brilliant, just like Andrea had said. His brain was like his office, jammed with facts and ideas, and, like his computers, he analyzed things with blinding speed that left me standing with my mouth open, like someone in the street who'd missed his bus. He saw things in the stories I described, even if he hadn't read them, and when I thought about what he said I realized he was right. At other times he seemed bewildered and helpless, like a kid lost in a big park. And at still others, when he was way down, he'd move and speak like a zombie, unconnected to the world. He'd get me down, too. On those days I didn't stay long.

Although we were different in every way, we had one thing in common. We didn't fit in.

Cutter was full of contradictions. He thought They got into his computers and monitored his phone calls, yet he had a lock on his mailbox. If They could watch him electronically, I reasoned, They could open his mail, couldn't They? And who steals mail, anyway? He knew They were after him because he exposed Their evil designs, but he faithfully took his meds (or said he did).

"Where do the meds come from?," I asked him once.

"The corps," he replied. "They use the dope to control me."

"But it's not working," I insisted. "You're after them."

"Exactly," he said, as if that made things clear. He knew the corps sent control signals from Buffalo—that was why he hung the disks in his windows, to deflect the waves. But when I asked him why he didn't find a doctor he trusted and have the chip removed from his brain, he waved his hand as if shooing away a fly.

"Tried that."

"So, what happened?"

"The nice doc assured me there was no electronic device lodged in my grey matter. Showed me an X-ray." Cutter smiled his lopsided smile. "Told me that thinking there was something in my head was all in my head."

"And you didn't believe it."

"Why should I? They're all in on it."

How do you reason with someone like that?

If you weren't careful, you'd think that Cutter didn't notice much, because he often seemed unfocused. But he observed things and stored the information away like a squirrel collecting nuts for winter. One time, just as I had finished unloading his dishwasher, he took my hands in his and examined the backs of my fingers.

"They healed up okay," he said.

I pulled away. "Huh? What do you mean?"

"Skinned knuckles. Swollen hands. I noticed a while back, when you were giving me my mail. You must have been in a fight."

"What if I was?" I said, hanging a towel on a rack under the sink. An image of the anger on Eileen's face flashed in my mind.

"Do you fight a lot?"

"Only when I have to. It's not like I go looking for it." Which wasn't really true. When I had been trying to get into the Tarantulas I had done exactly that.

"Do you like it?"

"No. I don't know. What kind of a question is that?"

"Just wondered. Because, you know, there are other ways to solve problems. Have you thought about why you choose violence?"

Cutter's tone was neutral. Not like he was judging me. He spoke as if he was asking about the weather. But I still didn't like the interrogation.

"What's it to you, anyway?"

He looked away, then lowered his head.

"No offense," I added stupidly.

Cutter almost never looked me directly in the eye, but he did then. "Lee, you're better than that," he said.

I finished my coffee, stashed my cell phone and notebook in my bag and, on my way through to the back door, dropped the mug into the dishwasher in the kitchen. In the courtyard behind the café, the big pots blazed with blossoms I didn't know the names of. I pushed the tank out into the alley, locked the door, mounted up, and pedalled over to Abe's house.

TWELVE

THE OLD TOWN HALL was a brick box squatting at the corner of 8th Street and the Lakeshore. I locked the tank to the pipe railing at the rear door, went inside, and took the steps to the second floor. I followed the corridor to the end, where gold letters on frosted glass announced LAKSHMI SMITH AND ASSOCIATES.

Inside were a desk, a couple of ratty-looking chairs, and a coffee table holding up a stack of magazines. A coat rack stood between a grimy window and a closed door. Behind the desk, a thin, grey-haired woman with a gold chain looped from her reading glasses around her neck was arranging files in a drawer. I stood at the desk until she decided to notice me.

"How may I help you?" she said, looking me up and down as if I had fallen off the back of a garbage truck.

I held out the big envelope Abe had given me. "Delivery for Lakshmi," I said.

"I trust you mean Ms. Smith," she sniffed.

"All I know is, Abe Krantz told me to bring this to Lakshmi," I told her.

"Ah, yes. The famous Mr. Krantz," she mumbled, taking the envelope from me.

"And he said Lakshmi—Ms. Smith—wanted me to deliver something."

"And you are?" she asked in a snotty voice.

"Lee," I said. "And you are?"

Behind her half-moon glasses, her eyes flared for a half-second. Her mouth puckered, as if she was holding back a burp.

"I am Mrs. Smith," she announced.

"Her mother?"

"Her mother-in-*law*, if it's any of your business," she snapped.

"Must be a bitch working for your daughter-in-law," I commented. It was none of my business, and I really didn't care, but the old bat was getting under my skin.

She pushed an envelope almost identical to Abe's across the desk. "The address is on the front."

I picked it up and waited.

"Was there anything else?"

"Five bucks, up front," I replied.

She shook her head, rattling the gold chain, took a bill from her purse and handed it over like a piece of lint she'd plucked from her sleeve.

"Do have a nice day," she said.

After I dropped Lakshmi's package off at another lawyer's office in Long Branch, Cutter called me on the cell.

"Can you pick up some mail, Lee?"

"Sure. Be there in a few minutes."

"Don't take your usual route," he said.

Cutter hadn't shaved yet or changed out of his pajamas and robe. He locked up behind me, avoiding my eyes. The printer was churning out pages. The shredder had been working overtime. A package sat on a table, balanced on a pile of file folders, duct-taped within an inch of its life.

Cutter led me into the kitchen. "Can you make some tea?" he asked, his voice small and raspy.

I set about filling the kettle and rinsing the teapot. "How's it going?"

"Fine, yeah, fine," he lied, his eye twitching. He ran his fingers through greasy hair, sat down and began to dry-wash his hands.

"Lee, you're my best friend," he said, looking up at me.

I shrugged my shoulders, felt a hot flush creeping into my face. "Can I make you something to eat?"

"No. Can't hold anything down today. Put some honey in the tea. Never mind, I don't have any honey. Don't even like the stuff." His voice rose to a shout. "I got them dead to rights, Lee!"

I sat at the table across from him. Sometimes, I had found, it was better to play along with him until I found out what was itching. "That's good," I replied. "So you're sending off your results in the mail?"

"Results, yeah, results. In the mail. See, I put it all together. They won't like my findings. I'm in the shit, now."

Cutter never swore. He was more than upset. He was scared. I wondered if I should call Andrea.

"Someday, Lee, the world will be ruled by the corps.

They've already gained enough power to influence govern-ments—the corps call it partnership—and democracy is almost dead, but in the near future they'll have taken over completely. Look at the wars of the last fifty years," he went on, calmly, resigned, "they were all fought for money. All for the benefit of the corps."

The kettle whistled and I got up, dropped a couple of teabags into the pot and poured the water in. I took two mugs down from the cupboard and put them on the table.

I took a chair. "Go on," I said. I figured if he kept talk-ing he might work himself loose from whatever had hold of him.

"They taught us in school," Cutter went on, "that wars were fought to end evil, or to spread democracy, but it was all lies. Wars were fought for silk and tea, spices, gold, dia-monds. Nowadays it's oil and gas and minerals."

He seemed to run down, like a CD player with a dying battery. He stared into his mug. I tried to make small talk, but he seemed to have slipped away somewhere.

Finally I went into the office. Cutter followed me. I picked up the package. It was addressed to the Secretary-General of the United Nations. At the door, I said, "Maybe you need some sleep." I didn't know what else to suggest.

His voice was a notch above a whisper. He stared at the floor between us. "There are more than fifty wars going on somewhere in the world, right this minute," he said.

He took my hand and shook it. "I'll see you, Lee," he said. Then he smiled and added sadly, "I was a peacekeeper, once." He closed the door softly behind me.

As soon as I turned the corner, I phoned Andrea and told her I was worried about Cutter. She said she'd call his doctor. He wasn't due for more meds, yet, Andrea said. Maybe he was just having a bad day.

"He's worse than bad," I said.

"People like Bruce are like that," she said. "They just have to ride it out."

I wasn't satisfied, but what did I know? What could I do? As if she was reading my mind she added, "The people around the person want to help, but sometimes there's nothing *anybody* can do."

I took his package to the post office. I didn't see him or hear from him for over a week. He wasn't answering his phone. I knocked on his door a couple of times. It was as if he'd gone away.

THIRTEEN

"THIRTY-ONE!" I CROWED, and scooped up the pennies from the middle of the table.

Reena threw down her cards. "I swear, if I didn't have *bad* luck I wouldn't have any luck at all."

"Stop complaining," I said. "You won the deal. And you shouldn't swear."

She blew her cigarette smoke in my direction. "Thanks for the advice, Father Mercer."

An hour or so earlier, Reena had called up to my room, where I was sprawled on the bed reading *A Farewell to Arms*. I still hadn't put enough money aside for my TV. "Wanna come down and lose some of that extra money you've been making?" she hollered. "There's nothing on TV and I'm out of magazines."

So we sat at the kitchen table under the fan, with the window open wide to catch whatever stray breeze wandered down 18th Street. A few wilted fries sat on a plate beside a beach of salt. Reena dealt a new hand.

I picked up my three cards, arranged them, and banged the table, making the pennies jump.

"You're knocking already?"

"Yup."

"Kids nowadays," she said.

She drew a card from the deck, squinted at it, and tossed it down with disgust. "I got eighteen."

"Too bad. Thirty for me."

I collected the pot—all ten pennies of it. The loser of the match had to spring for a take-out pizza. From upstairs came a chirping sound.

"What's that?" Reena asked.

"I changed the ring tone on my cell," I replied. "It's supposed to sound like a tree frog."

"A tree frog. Which has what to do with telephones?"

I got up from my chair. "I'll let you know when I've answered it."

I climbed the stairs quickly, wondering who would call at ten o'clock at night. I hoped it was Cutter. I still hadn't heard from him.

"Lee? It's Abe."

Abe Krantz didn't sound like his usual merry self. His voice was low and cautious. It wasn't about the weather this time.

"Hi, Abe. What's up?"

"Um, this pal of yours, Bruce. Does he live on 13th?"

"Yeah." Why was Abe calling about Cutter? As far as I knew, they'd never met.

Abe mentioned the house number. "Yup, that's him," I said. "What's this—?"

"I don't want to alarm you, Lee. But I just picked something up on the scanner. You might want to get over there."

"I'm on my way."

"Take the cell with you. I'll be here."

I skidded to a stop across the road from Cutter's house and let the tank fall against a hedge. A cluster of cop cars along with an ambulance clogged the street, their roof lights blipping across the fronts of the buildings. Radios squawked. Cops milled around. One uniform pushed back the small crowd that had formed, another was unrolling yellow Do-Not-Cross tape to form a perimeter around the front yard and driveway. Cutter's front door was open and I could see flashlight beams jumping around inside. I pushed through the onlookers and ducked under the tape.

"Hey!" A uniform rushed forward and put her hand on my chest. "Get back on the other side of the tape."

"My friend lives here," I said. "I've got to—"

"Do as I say! Now!" she said, shoving me back.

I knocked her arm aside, felt the buzz of adrenaline. "I told you—"

My phone chirped. "Lee? Abe. Are you there, yet?"

"They won't let me across the line," I said.

"Calm down. Tell me what's happening."

"I don't know!" I shouted. "It's a madhouse! There's cops and—"

Abe's voice became very harsh and firm. "Tell me what you see."

I described what was going on, which as far as I could tell was nothing but noise and confusion.

"They haven't come out of the house yet?"

"No."

"Now, listen. The cops have to follow procedure. They won't let anyone past the tape, except maybe a relative. Ask one of the uniforms who's in charge. See if you can get whoever that is to talk with you. Got it?"

"Yeah, but—"

"Take a deep breath and repeat what I just told you."

I went over Abe's instructions. Talking to him calmed me down a bit. I waited, straining to see into the house. Why didn't they turn on the lights? What were the cops doing in Cutter's house, and where was he? When Cutter found out the authorities were in his office, he'd go right over the edge.

Unless, I thought with a terrible sinking in my gut, he's already gone over the edge and barricaded himself in a room, ranting about conspiracies.

I called Reena to tell her what was happening. She began asking questions. "I gotta keep the line clear," I said, and cut her off.

The waiting was agony. Around me, neighbours whispered excitedly among themselves.

"Who lives there, anyway?" someone asked.

"I don't know," another answered. "Some guy. I've only seen him once or twice since he moved in."

"Whatever happened," a woman commented from behind me, "it ain't good."

Maybe Cutter isn't even there, I thought. That's why I haven't heard from him. He went away someplace. Maybe there's a gas leak or backed-up sewer inside.

A look around smashed my pathetic theories. There were no emergency vehicles other than the police cars and the ambulance. Its rear doors hung open, with no paramedics in view. The cops had been inside for a while. Cutter must be in there, too.

Finally, a man in a suit jacket came out onto the verandah. A badge was clipped to his jacket pocket. He came down the steps and along Cutter's sidewalk, flanked by two uniforms.

"Hey!" I shouted. "I got information you need."

The plainclothes cop, a tall skinny guy with wire-rimmed glasses, peeled off a pair of medic's gloves. "Who are you?" he asked.

"I know the guy who lives here. What's going on?"

"What's his name?"

"Bruce Cutter."

"Are you and him related?"

"No. He has no relatives here. He lives alone."

He ducked under the yellow tape. "Let's get in the car," he said.

He led me to an unmarked car with a revolving red light sitting on the dash. We got in and he turned off the light and tossed it behind him onto the back seat. He spoke into his radio for a bit, dropped the handset onto the seat, then turned to me. Asked me to identify myself, give my address.

"You say you know Mr. Cutter."

I swallowed and nodded.

"Would you say you were close?"

"Yeah," I replied. Then I added, "Very."

"I'm sorry to have to tell you this. We can't be sure yet, but it looks like suicide."

PART TWO

CUTTER

"And this also," said Marlow suddenly,
"has been one of the dark places of the earth."

—Joseph Conrad, *Heart of Darkness*

ONE

Autumn swept away the summer heat and brought a blaze of orange and yellow to the maples in the park across the Lakeshore, and new rhythms to the neighbourhood. Droves of students spilled out of streetcars and buses, and the café tables reserved for the street people filled up again as the weather cooled.

I didn't go to school that fall. Reena was disappointed. I wasn't ready for another big change in my life, I explained. I liked my job at the café, and I enjoyed getting out on the tank every day. I wanted things to stay the same for a while. She said she understood.

I was pedalling against the wind along Symon Street in Mimico one afternoon after a drug delivery, when the phone chirped. I pulled up at the curb.

"It's Mrs. Smith speaking."

"Yeah?"

There was a pause. "I see your manners haven't improved at all."

"I'd hate to disappoint you," I said.

"Are you able to come to the office at one o'clock?"

I looked at my watch. "Sure."

"Don't be late," she said.

"I'm never late," I said, but she had hung up.

Sharp on time I found cheery old Mrs. Smith behind her desk, jabbing stamps into a damp sponge before pressing them onto envelopes.

"Got a package for me?" I asked.

"Take a seat. Ms. Smith will be with you momentarily." She picked up her phone, stabbed a button, and announced my presence.

"Go on in," she ordered, and went back to assaulting the outgoing mail.

I had met Lakshmi a couple of times. She was a tall dark-skinned woman with a wide smile and a way of talking that didn't fit the businesslike image that her mother-in-law tried to project. She was sitting behind her desk, a telephone headset on, tapping a pencil on a file folder as she talked. When she saw me, she waved me to a chair.

Her office was small and totally unlike the lawyer's pads you see on TV. No thick carpet on the floor, no wood panelling, no liquor cabinet. Lakshmi was wearing leather jeans and a shirt rather than a business suit. She ended her call and pulled a file out of a drawer.

"Nice to see you, Lee," she said.

"You, too."

"How have you been?"

"Fine."

She was working up to something, but what? Lakshmi had never invited me into her office before. Maybe she wasn't satisfied with the service. Probably she was going to criticize or fire me for mouthing off at her mother-in-law.

"Lee, I asked you to come by because I need to discuss something with you."

I braced myself, ready to get up and leave the office. "Okay."

"You were a friend of Bruce Cutter's."

"Um, yeah," I said. How did she know? "So?"

"I'm—was—well, I guess I still am, his lawyer."

I looked at the wall above her head, losing focus. Unwelcome thoughts about Cutter and his self-murder came flooding back. Why had he done it, I had asked myself time and time again. And as many times, stung by guilt, I had gone over my last visit to his house, second by second, raking for clues that I should have picked up on, hints that he was getting ready to pack it in. He had shaken hands with me. At the time I had thought it was just Cutter being his unusual self. Should I have known what he was planning?

After a while, the shock of what he had done to himself had given way to an aching emptiness. He was, I realized after he was gone, the only real friend I had ever had. At the same time, I hated him because he had taken that friend away from me. Whenever Cutter barged into my mind I wanted to hit something.

"Lee?"

"Sorry," I said. Then added, "I didn't realize you knew each other."

"We go back a ways, since he moved into the neighbourhood a few years ago. He was one of my first clients. I handled all his business and personal affairs."

"Oh."

"But in spite of that, I knew very little about him. He was very, er, secretive."

Images of locks and bars and covered windows passed through my mind. "He sure was."

"I also handle his estate," Lakshmi added. "Which is why I need to talk with you."

She straightened up and opened a file. Her voice took on a firmer tone.

"Lee, this document is Bruce Cutter's last will and testament. You know what that is."

"Sure. But what's that got to do with me?"

"It names you as a beneficiary. My duty here today is to inform you of Bruce's wishes, explain the implications, and answer any questions you might have. It's taken a long time to get things in order because of the, well, unusual nature of his death. After I've gone over everything, I'll give you a document that outlines your inheritance in detail. Other documents relevant to the bequest will follow."

I fell back in my chair. "I didn't get any of that," I said. "Bruce left me something?"

"Yes."

"Why?"

"I can't speak for him, Lee. But you were his friend. Now, let me go through the details. Stop me any time you wish. Ready?"

Not ready, I almost said. I didn't want anything from him. I wanted him puttering around his office, guarding his garbage, ransacking the Net for data on the corps. I wanted him not to be dead.

"The bequest divides itself into two categories," Lakshmi began. "Real property and securities. The house on 13th Street and its contents are yours, free and clear. All taxes and insurance and utilities are paid up for this calendar year. Okay so far?"

I hadn't taken in a word, but I nodded anyway.

"There are some low-risk investments, earning enough interest to keep up the house, and to further your education, if you wish. It's held in trust until you're eighteen, at which time it comes to you in its entirety. But I am instructed to disburse reasonable amounts to you as and when you wish. You only have to tell me ahead of time so I can make arrangements."

Lakshmi closed the file and linked her fingers together on top of it. "I know this is pretty hard to absorb at first, Lee. I'm here any time you have a question. Bruce made it clear he wanted me to shepherd you along if necessary."

I nodded again, my head fogged in, my throat thickening. Cutter had given me his house? Money? Why?

Lakshmi pushed two envelopes across her desk. On top of them was a ring thick with keys. I stood, picked them up, shook hands with her, and left the office. In the parking lot at the rear of the building, I stuffed the envelopes and keys into my jacket pocket, unlocked the tank, and pedalled toward the café.

Along the Lakeshore, I rode as if I had somehow passed into what Cutter used to call Never-Never Land. Nothing made sense. Except that my friend was dead, and I felt as if I had stolen something from him.

———

I kept the inheritance to myself, mostly because I wanted time to wrap my mind around it. The keys and unopened envelopes lay in a drawer in my dresser. Every once in a while I'd remember that, according to Lakshmi, I owned a house. I had money. Which in my neighbourhood meant I was rich. But I still couldn't believe all that was real. So I continued to plod through my routines, going through the motions—as I had since the night I got Abe's phone call.

Near the end of October, Indian summer glided into the neighbourhood for a few days. On Sunday morning I picked up my book from my dresser, planning to take it down to the marina in the park, sit on a bench in the sun and relax—if I could. I was halfway down the stairs when I reversed direction, returned to my room and pulled open the dresser drawer. I tucked the envelopes between the pages of my book, pocketed the keys, and headed for the lake.

I took a bench by a small lagoon. Canada geese squabbled among themselves out on the water. Ducks squatted on flat rocks at the edge, heads tucked under their wings. In-line skaters, joggers, parents pushing baby carriages, came and went on the bike path. Dogs pulled their owners across the grass.

I tried to read my book, but gave in to curiosity. Both envelopes had Lakshmi's letterhead on them. The first contained one sheet with her signature, saying pretty much what she had told me in her office, only in more legal language. The second held a hand-written note.

Lee,

If you're reading this, Lakshmi has explained everything. Try to forgive me for what I've done; and try not to feel bad. I never did plan to stay around for too long.

Do what you want with the stuff in the house.

—Cutter

P.S. Don't forget to lock up.

I laughed when I read the last line. I folded the letter and the note and put them back in their envelopes. And then, for a long time, I looked out over the lake to the faint line in the distance where the water met the sky.

TWO

I had been doing a lot of work for Abe Krantz lately, delivering his take-out and shuttling documents back and forth to his clients—it's faster than the mail, he told me, and it makes the old folks feel important.

One day I found him sitting under a table umbrella on his back lawn, puffing a cigar and reading. Behind him, the propeller on his weather station turned lazily. I put his package on the table and, as always, he invited me to sit for a while. But first I went inside, fetched a lemonade for myself, filled an ice bucket for him, and collected his scotch from his office.

"What's it about?" I asked, pointing to the thick volume on his lap.

Abe was refusing to admit summer was gone. He was wearing checked Bermuda shorts and a striped T-shirt that showed he had once been a muscular guy, but had rounded off. I set down the tray of drinks and poured him a scotch and added ice.

He took a sip and sat back. "Ah, the staff of life," he said, his voice a low growl.

"If you say so."

"Where would civilization be without scotch and cigars?"

"Sober and cancer-less?"

He laughed. "Anyway, to answer your question, this book is about weather and history."

"Why the dinosaurs died off—stuff like that?"

"More like, the reason General So-and-so lost the battle of Such-and-such was because of the unexpected blizzard. Or, the rainy weather brought out more than the usual number of mosquitoes, which upped the incidence of malaria among the troops, which depleted the army, which delayed the invasion, which—"

"I think I get it. The whole book is like that?"

"Yup."

"Your hobby, the weather—you're a little like Cutter was," I said. "He was really analytical."

"Oh?"

"Yeah. He invented a computer game and, well, I haven't played it, but it's based on solving riddles and puzzles. And he did tons of research, put it together to make theories. Sometimes they made sense. Cutter was really smart."

Abe nodded. The breeze off the lake flapped the fringes of the umbrella. It felt good, cool and fresh, on my skin.

"It's tough, losing a friend," Abe said quietly.

"Yeah."

"My wife, Helen, she was my best friend."

When he raised his glass to his mouth, his hand was shaking.

Even though it was mine, now—Lakshmi had sent me all the documents to prove it—I stayed away from the house on 13th Street, with its darkened windows and haunted atmosphere. When a delivery took me to the area, I avoided the block between the Lakeshore and Morrison Street. I was scared to go into the place. Cutter had died there. He had gulped down a jar of sleeping pills, fallen back on his bed, and drifted away forever.

Why had he given me his house? What was I supposed to do with it? Did he expect me to move in? Did he even *know* why he had left me his home? After all, as he had told me himself many times, "I'm cracked."

I thought about it a lot as I pedalled around town, or peeled potatoes for the soup of the day, or emptied the café dishwasher—or when I lay sleepless in the middle of the night. After a while, I told Reena about my inheritance and asked her if she thought I should just sell the house and be done with it. She said to wait a while, not to make any decisions yet.

And then it occurred to me that if Cutter did have a reason for giving me his house—if it hadn't been just an irrational flash in his brain but part of a plan—the answer would be in the house itself. And the only way to find out was to push aside my fear and go there.

It was a cold, dreary afternoon, just after Reena had hung the CLOSED sign on the café door, when I mounted the tank and pedalled off to 13th Street, the ring of keys like a rock in my pocket. The rain, driven by the wind, lashed my face like sleet, and by the time I reached the house I was wet and shivering. The front yard was spattered with sodden leaves.

The red light glowing on the video camera over the front door gave me the creepy feeling that someone still lived there. I fished out the keys and fumbled through the bunch until I had the locks undone, and went inside, careful to lock up again. Then I shook my head, mumbled to myself, and unlocked the doors, determined not to fall into Cutter's paranoia. I made a mental note to bring extra rings with me next time so I could separate the keys into categories.

The place was so quiet I could hear the kitchen clock ticking. I found the light switch and suddenly I was back in the familiar, messy world of Cutter's office. Little red and green lights along the desk top told me the computers and peripherals had never been switched off, and the TV monitors showed the four outside locations covered by the cameras. I had never noticed before, but Cutter had rigged them to rotate the images through the four monitors, probably to prevent the images from burning the screens.

The house was warm and stuffy, with an underlying odour in the air. The smell grew stronger as I entered the kitchen. I looked under the sink and pulled out a sack of stinking potatoes in an obscene tangle of white shoots.

I took a plastic garbage bag and dumped the potatoes inside. In the fridge I discovered a container of yogurt giving off a powerful stench, some limp celery, a few wilted carrots, and half a cheese sandwich. All of it went into the garbage with the potatoes.

I tied up the bag and unlocked the back door. In the garage I found a garbage pail and tossed the bag inside. I saw a lawn mower, a trimmer, a rake, a few shovels, a couple of fuel cans. Cutter didn't own a car.

I went back inside and began to clean up the kitchen. The sense that I didn't belong in the house was like a voice nagging in my ear, but I kept going, forcing myself to finish what I had come for. I washed the countertop, the table, and the floor. I wiped down the shelves and walls inside the fridge. I emptied the dishwasher and stacked the dishes in the cupboards.

As I was hanging a towel over one of the chairs to dry, my cell chirped. It was Andrea.

"Are you free for a delivery, Lee?"

I thought about my plan to force myself upstairs to take a look around. Cutter's room—the place where he'd killed himself—was up there.

"Perfect timing," I said into the phone. "Be right there."

THREE

I was on the move all the next day and didn't get to Cutter's until after supper. This time I was determined not to let the place beat me, even though I was going in after dark. Once inside, I kept telling myself, you can't tell if it's day or night, anyway.

I went first to the basement. It was well lit, dry and uncluttered. The furnace rumbled away in one corner next to an old table and a half-dozen broken chairs. There was a shower stall beside the water heater, its taps and shower-head crusted with lime deposit. The door on the washing machine was flipped up, and a sock drooped over the lip of the open dryer door like a hound's tongue. All the windows were covered with black cloth tacked to the frames.

Back on the main floor, I thought I'd start a kind of inventory of all the stuff in the office. In a way I was interested to see some of Cutter's research. But I soon saw that it would take me ages to go through all the files piled on the tables. Hours to toss out the magazines. Days to examine all his printouts. Defeated, I sat down at the desk and flipped through the address book beside the phone. The handwritten entries were neat, listing a yard service, grocery delivery, contact numbers for telephone, natural gas, electricity accounts, my cell number, the pharmacy, the café. Beside the telephone company information was a pencilled note, "They're in on it!"

There were three PCs. I wasn't an expert, but it was obvious they were pretty new and, knowing Cutter, probably state-of-the-art. One seemed to be used only for Internet service. I took a quick look through the hard drive and found no applications other than internet software. Cutter had disabled the e-mail function on his browser and there was no stand-alone e-mail application. Why, I wondered. The bookmarks on the browser showed sites for news services in Toronto, New York, London, Manchester, and other cities around the world, along with a huge file of human rights sites, one folder labelled "Conspiracy Theories—Credible" and another, "Conspiracy Theories—Dumb." I wondered how goofy a conspiracy theory would have to be before Cutter would reject it.

The second computer had a few applications—word processing, an encyclopedia, spreadsheets and related stuff, and Cutter's banking records. The money files were all encrypted. No surprise there.

Games, lots of them, were the only function of the third computer. I knew nothing about games, so I didn't recognize any of the titles. I opened one file on the desktop titled "Peace. Game?" and saw only page after page of code.

According to the file's date, Cutter hadn't worked on it for more than a year.

I sat back and thought. Why had Cutter divided his activities between different machines? Wasn't it possible—easy, for him—to put everything on one computer? I remembered him saying something about being naked in a glass house when you used the Internet. Was that the reason? Did he think that separating his work would protect it somehow? I decided I would never know the answer, so I shut down the PCs and turned off the peripherals, the monitors, and VCRs connected to the CCTV cameras. I wondered what to do next.

The stairway to the left of the vestibule door led to the upper floor. The darkness beyond the top step gave me the creeps. I took a deep breath, flicked the switch, gripped the banister, and forced myself to climb. As I went, every stair creaked.

I found myself in a hallway. A window on the back wall of the house was covered. The hall led toward the front of the house, where black curtains hid another window. There were three doors. In the bathroom a toothbrush poked from a glass on the sink, a squashed tube of toothpaste beside it, the cap missing. An electric razor dangled from a socket at the end of its cord. A couple of rumpled towels lay on the floor.

The door leading to Cutter's bedroom was open. I stuck my head inside. A double bed, the blankets jumbled and skewed, a night table with a small lamp, a dresser, an easy chair beside a covered window. Good enough, I thought, closing the door.

The one remaining door had been secured by three big padlocks. The key ring jangled as I released each one.

I pushed the door open, flipped the switch, and lit up a nightmare.

The ordinary furniture—a desk, a trestle table cluttered with files, and a few filing cabinets—seemed out of place in a room that screamed insanity. The ceiling, floor, and walls—even the glass in the single window—had been painted flat black, and seemed to press in on me. Opposite the door, the entire wall was plastered with glaring orange, yellow and red graffiti, the letters jagged and sharp. MOOTWA SHALL INHERIT THE EARTH dominated the space.

I stepped around the desk and took a closer look. The window had been nailed shut. All the graffiti had been written in chalk. All the phrases were multi-coloured, some, like the banner, a foot high, some as small as four inches. Mistah Kurtz, he in Kijevo! The schoolyard is mined!! Operation HARMONY?!! Karlovac is the rabbit hole! Tell Alice! and, in vermilion, They killed them ALL!!

I don't know what it was—the claustrophobic atmosphere of the little room with the black wall, the glaring words that had erupted from an insane mind, the violence of each letter with its points and jagged edges, the certainty that Cutter had spent hour after hour, bent over or kneeling on the hardwood floor, maniacally working sharpened bits of chalk back and forth like a demented prisoner—but the room seemed to scream out "Run!"

And run was exactly what I did. I stumbled down the stairs and out the door and into the clear, cold, normal autumn night.

FOUR

ALTHOUGH I HAD TOLD Reena about my inheritance, asking her to keep it to herself, she didn't know that I had visited Cutter's house a couple of times, so one day I filled her in. We were unpacking the early morning delivery from the food wholesaler's. "I just don't know where to start," I said, "or what I should do."

Reena pulled open the flaps of a large carton and began placing celery stalks, tomatoes, carrots and onions on the long bench opposite the dishwasher. She tossed the empty carton toward the back door, leaned on the counter and lit a cigarette.

"After your grandma went into the home," she began, "and your dad and I knew she'd never come back to her house on Harvie Street, I was in the same boat. Your dad was all tied up with your mom's illness at the time, and taking care of you, so the job fell to me."

She flicked her cigarette ash into the sink. I began to dice carrots.

"So," she continued, her face suddenly softer, "I guess I can relate to what you're saying. It's a terrible job, having to go through someone else's stuff—a lifetime of possessions and clothes and memories. Keepsakes and junk. You feel like you're invading their home. And throwing someone else's possessions away—someone you love—seems sacrilegious. Like you're attacking them, stealing from them, and they're not there to defend themselves. And at the same time you know that you're doing it for them, that you'd never allow a stranger to go through the house and clean it out. It's a duty, and you want to do it, but at the same time you feel like a creep.

"I remember, I got most of the job done—it took four or five days—and then I found a box at the back of Mom's closet, the kind Christmas cards come in. It was stuffed so full she had knotted a ribbon around it to hold the lid on. Inside were all the anniversary cards Dad had given her over the years, all the birthday greetings, and two congratulations cards from when your dad and me were born, each one signed 'Love, Doug.' A whole lifetime in a box held together with a bit of tattered ribbon."

Reena wiped her eyes with the back of her hand. "What the hell do you do with a box of old cards?" she said.

She picked up another carton, turned her back and began to stack packages of cheese and sliced meat on the counter. I chopped more vegetables. A while later I asked, "So, what did you do with it?"

Reena's tough manner was back. "Ah, it's upstairs somewhere," she said.

———

"Every once in a while," Abe said, "I come to the conclusion that, on the whole, life makes sense, then something like this comes along."

We were in his work room. Classical music played softly in the background. Abe sat in a leather chair, an empty glass balanced on the arm, his feet on a hassock. I sat in his desk chair.

Although I had gotten nothing practical from her, Reena had made me feel better about things. She understood, and I don't know why exactly, but knowing she understood lightened the weight I had carried on my shoulders since the day Lakshmi whacked me on the head with the news of Cutter's will. So I decided to ask Abe for advice.

I trusted him. I had liked him from the first day. He never talked down to me. And I had a lot of respect for him, especially after I found out that the bookkeeping and tax stuff I couriered back and forth to his "old folks" was all done for free. Mr. Chekowski, apartment 14B in the seniors' retirement residence in Mimico, had let the secret out of the bag. It wasn't Mr. Chekowski's fault. He was in his eighties and starting to lose his memory.

"See if you can put your problem into words for me," Abe said.

"All I have in my head are questions," I began. "Cutter must have had a plan. That's why he gave me his house and everything in it. But I can't figure out what it might be."

"This problem cries out for a Cohiba," Abe announced. "I got to smoke to think."

I got up and fetched a cigar from the rosewood humidor on Abe's desk. He clipped the end, dropped the nub into the ashtray, and leaned forward to the lighter I held for him. When he had puffed enough of a cloud to close an airport, he sat back again and looked at the ceiling.

"If you ever quit Reena, you could get a job as a butler. Anyway, maybe your friend was just nuts. Maybe there was no reason. Crazy people's actions aren't always, well, sane."

"You had to suck on a twenty-dollar cigar to come up with that brilliant conclusion?" I said.

He laughed. "I like that you're keeping a sense of humour about all this. No problem is ever so big that it can't be laughed at."

"Yeah, well, when I'm in that house, the last thing I feel like doing is laughing."

"Can't say I blame you. Okay, we look at this like it's a mystery that we need to solve."

"A conundrum." It was my word for the day.

"Exactly. If Cutter's actions are simply the product of a deranged mind, there's no answer. So, we set that possibility aside. What are we left with?"

Abe clamped the cigar in the corner of his mouth and ticked his index finger. "One, Cutter wanted you to do something." He ticked his middle finger. "Or, two, he wanted you to know something."

"Or," I said, "both."

The next time I unlocked Cutter's front door, a full pannier banged against my legs as I hauled it inside. I kicked off my snowy boots, went straight through to the kitchen and unpacked, laying everything out on the table. I had brought a dozen 100-watt lightbulbs, a screwdriver set with pliers, a flashlight, a new notepad, a small radio, and some sandwiches and coffee Reena had insisted on making for me. It was Sunday and I had all day.

My first move was a sacrilege, to use Reena's word. I dragged a chair to the kitchen window, climbed up, and yanked the curtains aside, producing a cloud of dust that swirled in the sunlight that suddenly poured into the room. I tugged the aluminum disks out of the window and dropped them on the counter.

Carrying the chair, I marched from room to room, pulling the drapes open and jerking down the disks. Then I climbed the stairs and freed the windows up there. With light coming in, Cutter's bedroom seemed less creepy. I stripped the linen from his bed, collected the towels from the bathroom, and hauled the whole lot downstairs to the garbage.

I propped open the door of the "crazy room," as I had come to call it, set my radio on one of the filing cabinets, and tuned it to a local rock station, turning the volume low. I cleared the desk, piling Cutter's books and files on the table, and climbed on top. One of the bulbs in the ceiling fixture was dead, the other only a 60-watt, so I replaced both of them with the stronger bulbs I had brought with me.

The bright light chased the shadows from the corners, but the wall with the manic graffiti seemed to shout even louder. The strange words, MOOTWA, Kijevo, Kurtz, Karlovac, blazed against the black background. Grunting with the effort, I turned the desk around so I wouldn't have to face the madness.

I opened my notepad, placed it on the desk, and began with the filing cabinets. In the first, all three drawers were packed with neatly labelled files. I flipped through a few. "International Monetary Fund" took up four inches, "Land Mines" another three, "Political Donations: Corporate" and "Privatization of Military" a whole drawer. Cutter's research. I wondered how many hours he had spent compiling all the information.

I pulled open the top drawer of the second cabinet. It seemed to be devoted to Cutter himself. There were records dating back to his days in elementary school, and more recent legal papers like insurance policies, a copy of the deed to the house, warranties for appliances, and a thick folder of documents relating to his video game. The first file in the middle drawer contained one sheet of paper with Department of National Defense on the letterhead. It was dated a month or so before Cutter killed himself. It was addressed to him, and said, "On December 1 at 08:00 hours, a ceremony will be held . . . ." I skipped down the page. It named a place, a stadium in Winnipeg. Why, I wondered, was the Department of Defense writing to Cutter? Somehow I couldn't imagine him, with his strange ways, part of an army, standing to attention or saluting or polishing his buttons. Or following orders.

But then I heard myself say, "Hey, wait a minute." The last time I had seen Cutter he had said something I let slip by because it meant nothing to me at the time. Fifty wars, he had told me, were raging right now, somewhere in the world. And then, "I was a peacekeeper, once."

There were more files concerning military stuff. And magazine and downloaded newspaper articles about investigations and commissions of inquiry into army matters. The dates stretched back over ten years.

In the bottom drawer I found three hardback notebooks. They were cloth-covered, scuffed and stained, the pages curled and dirty. I flipped one open. Neat handwriting filled the pages. Cutter's handwriting. The margins were covered with doodles, little drawings of houses, mountains, farm wagons. I opened another. The writing was more spidery, as if hurried. The black and red ink sketches showed tanks and rifles and bullets. In the third, scrawls punctuated by exclamation marks filled the pages, sometimes corner to corner rather than between the lines. And the drawings depicted skeletal faces, mouths stretched wide in horror, eyes missing, teeth broken.

I slammed the book closed, my heart racing, and went to push the drawer closed with my foot. Then I saw something. I set the books on the desk, got down on my hands and knees, and reached to the back of the drawer. My fingers scraped on metal. It was a helmet, light blue in colour. I set it on the floor and it wobbled a couple of times. I reached in again and brought out a wood-handled knife in a leather sheath. The knife was razor sharp. The last item was an old shoe. A child's leather shoe, scuffed, the heel worn down. One side and the toe were covered by a stain, dark, reddish-brown, blackening at the edges.

Blood.

By late that afternoon I had moved my centre of operations downstairs to the office. I cleared the trestle tables, piling the contents on the floor under the front window, and tidied the computer desk. I dug out Cutter's software disks and, while I held the cell phone to my ear, followed Abe's instructions, installing the encyclopedia and word-processor on the computer Cutter had devoted to Internet access so I'd have everything in one place. It would be my research headquarters. "Might as well add the mail program," Abe advised. "Then you can contact me that way, too, if you want. What's going on up there, anyway?"

"I'll let you know," I replied, "when I know."

I was fumbling in the dark. I had a powerful feeling that I was starting out on some kind of journey, not at all sure where I was going or how I would get there, but I knew the direction I'd take. There would be a lot of reading, a lot of thinking, a million pieces to put together. Probably false trails and dead ends. I had a ghost leading me.

I called Reena, told her I'd be home late. "You sound excited," she said. "What's up?"

"I think I'm onto something. Talk to you later."

I jotted down a list of words already burned in my brain. Kijevo, Kurtz, Karlovac, MOOTWA. I launched the computer's encyclopedia. Today was as good a day as any to begin.

"Hang on, Cutter," I said to the empty house. "I'm on my way."

PART THREE

MOOTWA

Oh for shame, how the mortals put the blame on us
gods, for they say evils come from us, but it is they, rather,
who by their own recklessness win sorrow beyond what is given.

—Homer, *The Odyssey*

ONE

CUTTER WAS AN "ONLY," like me. He was born in a little town called Pictou on the Northumberland Strait that separates Nova Scotia from Prince Edward Island. His parents ran the snack bar on the ferry that worked the crossing between nearby Caribou and Woods Island, PEI.

Cutter's school records showed a monotonous string of A's, from grade one through high school, with neat handwritten comments that praised his high marks and pointed out that he was a loner and seemed to be withdrawn at times. Except for the grades, I could have been reading about myself.

He got into the University of Toronto on a full scholarship and proceeded to knock off top marks and prizes in electrical engineering. Somewhere along the line he became a pacifist. He didn't believe war was noble or heroic. He thought it was insane.

WILLIAM BELL

From Cutter's diary, volume one

At the Somme in the First World War, a five month battle costing 415 thousand lives on the British side alone gained 45 square miles of empty ground. 45! That's 9 thousand dead for each square mile. How bad does it have to get before someone says, "Hey, wait a minute! This isn't worth it!" During the last two years of the Second World War, over a million people were being killed each month. Who could say with a straight face that the generals who directed such lunacy were in their right minds? If individual human beings acted the way nations or tribes at war behave, they'd be locked away as dangerous offenders.

In his first year of university he caught the computer game bug and by the middle of second year he was already designing his own games and thinking about signing up for the armed forces reserves, which seemed like a strange interest for a pacifist electronics genius with a bright future promising great jobs and lots of money. His mom and dad were against it. "Too dangerous," they said, in the letters that Cutter had kept. "You could get killed, Bruce, and then what would we do?"

His parents were driving home from the Caribou ferry wharf one night when a drunk driver wandered across the solid line, turning their pickup truck into scrap metal and making Cutter an orphan.

He began his diary when he signed up and became a "weekend soldier." It described his infantry training on weekends and holidays, and his hope that someday he'd

116

become a peacekeeper with the United Nations. He got top scores in marksmanship but had no intention of firing his weapon at another human being. "Fighting for peace," he wrote, "is like shouting for silence. I'm going to do MOOTWA, Military Operations Other Than War." A pacifist in the army. Typical Cutter.

In 1993 he heard that Canada planned to send forces to the Balkans as part of UNPROFOR, the United Nations Protection Force, and he volunteered. Yugoslavia was tearing itself to pieces, and the U.N. was trying to keep people from each other's throats.

From Cutter's diary, volume one

Balkan history is "Alice in Wonderland" with guns and death squads. Off with their heads! Our training lectures weren't much help. Had to do some reading.

Yugoslavia is about a quarter the size of Ontario. Used to be a country but after 1990 it broke up into the six nations that had formed it. A major problem was that the inhabitants of Yugoslavia didn't choose their homes according to lines on a map. There were Slovenians in Croatia, Croatians in Bosnia, and Serbians everywhere. Serbia is the strongest of the six, and wants to dominate the rest "For its own protection." When Croatia, which is smaller than New Brunswick, voted for separation (also "For its own protection") the murderous war for "Greater Serbia" began to rip the place apart.

Serbs and Croats speak dialects of the same language. In appearance there's nothing to distinguish one from the other. Croats are Roman Catholic Christians. Serbs are

Eastern Orthodox Christians. Croats write using Latin script. Serbs use Cyrillic writing, like the Russians. The two ethnic groups got along for years until the priests and politicians began to have their way and neighbour was turned against neighbour. Newspapers on each side accused the other of horrible crimes and screamed for revenge. Militias were formed. Drunks and criminals and fools were armed and sent on missions.

What happened in Kijevo tells it all. It's a village in Croatia inhabited by Croats, but situated in an area where the communities around it are mostly ethnic Serbian. One day, Kijevo was attacked by Serbs and "purified." The inhabitants were driven out or shot, the livestock was slaughtered and left to rot, the crops were burned, the wells were poisoned with dead animals or gasoline, the buildings were blown up and burned. Kijevo is the hellhole where they made up the term "ethnic cleansing."

We got off the plane in Zagreb and formed up in the icy rain. Hauled our gear into white U.N. buses, settled in for the three-hour drive to "sector west," where we'd be stationed.

The city fell away behind. We pushed deeper and deeper into a blasted landscape—village after village of pulverized buildings, collapsed roofs, bullet-pocked walls standing beside piles of rubble. Churches smashed and desecrated. Fields cratered and churned by artillery. Animal carcasses, bloated and rotting, in fields nobody could farm because of the land mines.

This is a war between villages. I don't understand it. A few years ago these people worked side by side in

factories, newspapers, offices. They bought seeds and fertil-
izer from one another. They played soccer together. They
intermarried.

What happened?

Possible answers to be investigated if I make it home
alive:

Satan happened.
Politicians and priests happened.
History happened.
God happened.

Cutter's platoon set up camp in a deserted village and began fortifying the walls with bags of dirt. Their mission was to keep the main road open, disarm the combatants, destroy weapons dumps, protect the citizens, keep the peace.

"What peace?" Cutter wrote. "This place is no-man's-land. Sniper fire. Skirmishes. Ambushes. Murders and retaliations. Ordinary people—and us—caught in the crossfire."

But a lot of the time, Cutter was bored. He spent his downtime reading, keeping his diary up to date, playing soccer with local kids, maintaining his equipment. He honed his jump master's knife whether it needed it or not, and oiled the leather scabbard. It had been made in Pictou, where he grew up.

From Cutter's diary, volume one

At a checkpoint on the "main road," Randall Cloud and
I were taking a break, sitting in the shade of our M113
playing chess on a miniature board. I was looking
around, waiting for Randall to make up his mind, when

I spotted a figure walking down the dirt road toward us. As he got closer I noticed he was hobbling, then the reason became clear. He was grasping a crutch with both hands so that his upper body was turned to the side, making his progress slow and awkward. He was ten, maybe twelve, but so skinny and malnourished he could have been sixteen. His T-shirt and shorts were ragged, the toes of his foot poked out of his shoe. He hitched right up to us and stood staring at the board, leaning on his crutch. His damaged leg had been sheared off below the knee, and the healed wound looked like melted plastic. In the distance, machine-gun fire broke out. Nobody turned to look.

By August Cutter was only a couple of months away from being sent home. He was looking forward to decent meals and peaceful university classrooms. Then his company was ordered to pack up and prepare to move out. The Croats were gearing up for a major offensive in the south. The Serbs had rearmed and reinforced in response.

In a "cleansed" village called Tamomir, Cutter's squad moved into in another abandoned house, its walls gouged by bullets and blackened by smoke. The village's name meant Over There is Peace. "Must be over there," Cutter scribbled. "Certainly isn't here!"

During a break on the second day, Cutter sat in the shade of the house studying his map. Sweat dripped from his forehead onto the plastic cover. The battlefront stretched roughly northeast–southwest. The Canadians, the only peacekeepers in the area, were near the Serb line. But between Tamomir, the Serb headquarters, and Gospic, the Croat centre of operations, the front ballooned like a weak spot in a blood vessel into Croat-held territory to the west. Inside this "Tamomir Bulge," were many ethnic Serb villages, and the Croats' objective was to capture the Bulge and "straighten out" the front. Everyone knew what that meant for the villagers.

There were rumours that Croats detained by UNPRO-FOR had been carrying satellite maps that could only have come from U.S. sources, that Germany was secretly supplying arms and even tanks to the Croat forces. And Russia was backing the Serbs.

"The Big Powers aren't fighting this war," Cutter wrote, "they're *catering* it!"

From Cutter's diary, volume two

When the attack came, I prayed.

Not for deliverance from death. Not for my comrades in arms. I chanted "Please, please, don't let me crap my pants." I was terrified that, if they found me dead and stinking, they'd think I was a coward, or if I survived, the guys would laugh.

It was 6:30 a.m. and I was squatting in the weeds behind the house, brushing my teeth out of a tin cup, when, blam! the first mortar bomb exploded some distance away. The second blast knocked me sideways under a rainstorm of red dirt and rocks. The pounding went on all day. The noise and the smell and the shaking of the ground scraped my nerves raw.

It was the Croats, we were told. They can't do that, I thought, we're the U.N. Then I laughed. You fool. We're in the Balkans.

The Croats pushed into the villages of the Bulge and began looting, destroying, and killing. On September 9, Cutter's squad moved into a field and dug in, close to the Croat line, which was hidden in the forest at the edge of the field. By placing themselves between the Serbs and Croats, the peacekeepers hoped to enforce a ceasefire. Then the Serb force drifted away. Cutter was checking his ammo when the lip of the berm at the edge of his trench seemed to explode and the rattle of machinegun fire rolled over him. His helmet was whacked by a shell and snatched away just as he ducked below ground. Up and down the Canadian line, fountains of dirt and mud sprang into the air. The peacekeepers were allowed to return fire if they were directly attacked. To his left and right, Cutter's mates opened up. Machineguns chattered, men yelled, calling out to each other, "Get them! Give it to 'em."

Cutter was in his first real firefight. Adrenaline buzzed through his veins. A hollowness socked his bowels. His hands shook on his rifle. He had been trained to kill the enemy, but had never had any intention of doing it. I'm a peacekeeper, he told himself as the air around him bloomed with smoke and cordite and rang with gunfire.

He sighted down his rifle barrel at the line of trees. Gun muzzles sparkled like camera flashes at a football game. Cutter fired into the trees, high above the flashes. I won't shoot at them unless they come out of the trees, he told himself. At the same time, he was conscious of his comrades. Were they as scared as he was? By failing to fire at the muzzle flashes as he had been trained to do, wasn't he letting them down? He knew some who would be excited.

Bursting with dammed-up frustration, they had been aching for a chance to fight.

The firefight raged through the night. Men scrabbled to and fro around Cutter, delivering ammunition and water. He heard the screams of Croats who had been hit. Torn by indecision, he found himself firing for effect one minute, shooting high the next, tears streaming down his face.

When dawn came, the Croat line fell silent, and as the light rose Cutter realized that they had melted away. During the night-long battle, no U.N. soldiers died, but almost three dozen Croats were killed. Cutter was sick with guilt.

As the peacekeepers moved into the Tamomir Bulge behind the retreating Croats, their mission changed again. First, they would distribute food, water, and blankets to the Serb civilians in the Bulge and gather them up so the U.N. could help them find somewhere else to live. Second, dead bodies were to be collected and transported to a temporary morgue for examination. Third, Cutter's platoon was ordered to help "gather and record" evidence of war crimes. RCMP officers had been brought from Canada to help.

"First assignment—easy," Cutter scrawled. "Second task—hard. The Croats left almost no one alive." Cutter's platoon started to move through the valleys, collecting evidence of atrocities and war crimes. On one farm they found a chicken coop still standing. Cutter wondered why it had not been destroyed along with the other buildings. He ducked into the low doorway and, in the dim light, made out the shadowy forms of two people sitting on chairs in the corner, facing him. "*Ne plaši se. Ja sam tu da ti pomognem*," he called out. "Don't be afraid. I'm here to help you." When his eyes had adjusted to the dimness, he stepped nearer.

Then he gasped and vomited onto the straw.

Blackened skulls, hung with strips of burned flesh, grinned at him. The two women had been tied to the chairs and set on fire.

Through the next week, hour by hour, Cutter's sanity slipped away. He found the corpse of an old woman lying in a field. She had been tortured and then shot in the head. On another farm, seven uniformed Serbs had been executed, dragged into a barn, covered with straw, and doused with gasoline. The straw had been too damp to burn properly. Further on, an old man, his face a pulp of bloody flesh, had been shot twenty-four times. Bodies of men and women were found. They had been tortured by knife and fire, then shot in the head.

And one warm autumn afternoon, when the sun lit up the red and gold oak forests on the mountains, Cutter and three other troops approached another smashed village. On the outskirts, somebody called a halt, pointing to an area of freshly churned-up ground. Cutter came upon a man's workboot lying on the ground and bent to pick it up. It was stuck in the dirt. He pulled harder, then realized the boot was still attached to a body. He called for the RCMP officer.

"Dig," he told them. "Looks like a mass grave."

They worked for hours but didn't find any more bodies, only a large number of bloody surgery gloves.

The Croats had dug up a bunch of corpses and moved them. To hide the evidence, the cop figured. Cutter, his stomach churning, folded his spade and turned away, glad to be finished with the job. Then he noticed something lying at his feet. It was a small shoe, the toe and one side stained with dried blood. He snatched it up and stuffed it inside his tunic, as if, in saving the shoe, he could bring the murdered kid back to life.

The next morning, Cutter didn't respond to reveille. When spoken to, he showed no awareness. His eyes stared into a distance only he could see. He was flown back to Canada, declared unfit for duty, and ignored by the Department of National Defense for nearly ten years.

One day, after Cutter had fought his way closer to a normal life in spite of the voices in his head and messages beamed from Buffalo, a letter arrived. I realized that I had probably retrieved it from the locked mailbox on his porch for him. The letter invited regulars and reservists who had served with the 2nd Battalion of the Princess Patricia's Canadian Light Infantry in Croatia in September 1993 to a ceremony where the battalion would receive a Governor General's Citation "for courageous and professional execution of duty." The new parade formation would be called "The Tamomir Guard."

There was no reason given for the fact that Canada had pretty much ignored the achievements of Cutter and his mates for nine years. The letter explained that Cutter would have to pay his own way to the ceremony.

I wondered, sitting in his now brightly lit office, his

blue, bullet-creased peacekeeper's helmet on the desk beside the bloodstained shoe, if Cutter had decided to end his life even before the Defense Department contacted him. Or had the letter pushed him to the bedroom across the hall and the container of pills? Or had he always, since coming home with his sanity in shreds, kept that option open, like a plane ticket tucked in a drawer, ready to be used when the time came?

And where did I come in? I thought I understood now what he had wanted me find out. "Now you know," I saw him saying, a crooked smile on his thin lips, "why I'm batty." He had travelled into the centre of a terrible darkness, he had seen what nobody should ever have to see, and he had never really made it back.

TWO

IT TOOK ME MORE than a month to put Cutter's story together, working at his desk, his files and journals close at hand. To understand the background better, I ransacked a few history books and printed off articles from the Net. More than once, as I found and fitted together bits of the puzzle, I told myself that I must look exactly like Cutter, obsessed by my quest. Reena and Abe Krantz held back their curiosity and tried not to badger me with questions.

Soon the Christmas season was blasting away, with carols on the radio day and night, warbling about peace on earth and pre-Christmas blowout sales. Reena had put up a sickly little plastic evergreen tree in the window of the café and hung a sign above the coffee bar saying HAPPY WHATEVER YOU CELEBRATE AT THIS TIME OF YEAR. She pretended to be a grinch or a scrooge, muttering about the

Christmas hype as she worked and smoked in the kitchen, but she set out extra muffins and cookies for the street people and let them hang around in the café's warmth longer than usual.

After the new year had rolled around, I left my bedroom one night and found Reena doing a crossword puzzle at the kitchen table. I sat down and, over a cup of tea, filled her in on Cutter's story. She listened intently, and when I was finished she said, "I wish I had known him better."

"Me, too," I replied.

January plodded along. The third week barrelled in on a blizzard that left the city paralyzed for three days. Abe had predicted it, telling me confidently, "It will last three days, not two, like they're saying on the radio." Once the snowplows had made a few swipes at the streets, I carried on as normal. At the beginning of December I had fitted the tank with new heavy-duty tires, so the snow didn't affect the Lee Mercer Courier Service. It melted off pretty fast, anyway.

Abe was a different kind of listener. Where Reena sat in silence, he interrupted a lot and questioned me on details, as if I was being interviewed. "Boy, you sure know your stuff," he said more than once before I finished.

"I learned a lot," I said.

"Is your mind resting a little easier now?"

"I don't know. I have to think some more."

"That's good," he said. "Thinking is good."

"The only name on the black wall I couldn't chase down was 'Kurtz.'"

"What did it say again?"

"'Mistah Kurtz, he in Kijevo.'"

"Well, we both know about Kijevo. Mistah like M-I-S-T-A-H?"

"Yeah."

"Hmm. I think that's in a poem. 'We are the hollow men/We are . . .'—No, wait. Originally, Kurtz is from a book."

Abe puffed a few times, head back in his chair, then took a sip of scotch. "Got it. Kurtz is a character in a novel. Long story short, he's a trader in central Africa and he learns that he's capable of extreme, almost total, evil and the knowledge drives him mad."

"That fits," I said. "'Kurtz is in Kijevo.' What happened there was certainly evil. What's the book's title?"

"The Heart of Darkness."

I nodded. "That fits, too. How come you know all this? I thought you were an accountant."

"Yes, but a literary accountant," Abe laughed.

"Not exactly normal," I commented. "Er, I mean ordinary."

"True. And, before you ask, no offense taken."

"Come to think of it, nobody I know is ordinary—you, me, Cutter. Reena isn't exactly typical, either."

"Maybe nobody is," Abe said.

After a while I said, "There was a time when I would have called a guy like Cutter a coward and a weakling."

Abe nodded and took a pull from his drink, but didn't say anything.

"Not any more," I said.

I pumped hard against a damp, chilly wind on my way home from an evening movie on Bloor Street, my front and rear safety lights blipping, tires shushing on the damp pavement. It was about 11:30, not a moon or a star in the sky. The traffic was light on 18th Street. I powered up the bridge over the Queen Elizabeth Way, and spun the pedals fast going down the other side, timing my approach to the traffic lights so I'd get a green, sailing through the intersection, coasting as far as I could before using my legs again. I made the lights at Horner, and at Birmingham, too.

When I swooped into the alley behind the café it was nearly midnight. I unlocked the back gate, pushed the tank ahead of me into the courtyard, and re-locked the gate, wishing that, just once, I could look at a lock and not think of Cutter.

I let myself in through the door as quietly as I could. Reena would likely be asleep by now. I hung my coat on the peg, slid off my wet boots, felt my way through the dark kitchen without turning on the lights, and crept up the stairs. From Reena's room I heard a thump, like a dresser drawer being closed, and when I saw the oblong of yellow light on the floor of the upstairs hall I knew she was still up. If her door was closed at night, it meant she was in bed. If not, she was watching TV or reading. On my way past her door, I popped my head in to say goodnight.

And saw, in profile, a tall, heavy man bent over an open dresser drawer, rummaging around inside.

I froze. My eyes darted around the room, seeking Reena. I caught sight of a slippered foot protruding from the far side of her bed. A fuzzy pink slipper.

The man jerked upright. He was unshaven, wearing a jacket with a dirty fleece collar and heavy work boots. He lunged for me, but caught his boot on the edge of the rug by Reena's easy chair, and fell. His head cracked the table by the chair, tossing the reading lamp the floor. He grunted as the air exploded from his lungs and lay there, dazed. I dropped to one knee and punched him on the temple as hard as I could. He groaned. I socked him again and he went limp.

I straddled him, yanked his arms behind him, and dragged the reading lamp toward me. I tore the electric cord loose and tied him tightly by the wrists, my knuckles already aching from the punches.

Reena lay sprawled on her stomach, her hair dishevelled, one arm caught under her body. I took her by the shoulders as gently as I could. She flinched, cried out, and tried to crawl away.

"Reena, it's Lee!" I said. "It's okay. He's gone."

Which wasn't true, but I couldn't think of anything else to say to calm her. She let me help her sit up.

"Can you stand?"

"Where's Del?"

"Don't worry about him. Come on, try to get to your feet."

I helped her up off the floor and sat her on the bed, pulling her bathrobe closed and knotting the belt. Her head hung down, hair falling forward to cover her face.

"Reena, are you all right? Look at me."

She raised her head. One eye was already purpling. A few strands of hair stuck to the blood that oozed from one nostril. Her lower lip had been split, and a crimson trickle leaked over her chin, dripping onto her chest. She breathed deeply through her mouth.

"Don't let him hit me any more," she gasped.

"Don't worry," I snarled.

In a black rage I stepped over to the man and grabbed him by his elbows, yanking them together and lifting. He had come around by then and as I hauled him out of the room he howled in pain. In the hall I dropped him, screamed, "Shut up!" and kicked him in the ribs. He let out another yelp. I latched onto him again and half lifted, half dragged him along the floor to the top of the unlit staircase, cursing, "You son of a bitch!" again and again.

"No, no, don't!" he moaned, twisting his head to look up at me, his eyes wide with terror. He was conscious enough to know what he was in for.

I let go of his arms, hooked one hand under the neck of his jacket, the other in his belt, and gathered my strength to throw him down the stairs. "Please! Don't!" he wailed. "Please!"

"Lee! Lee!" Reena cried from her room.

In that split second, my mind was jammed with sound—the man's begging, Reena's screaming, the rage roaring in my ears. I held the man over the dark well of the staircase, my legs braced against his weight, about to dump him, watch him tumble and bounce down the steps, breaking his bones and twisting his neck.

"Lee! What are you doing?"

I lowered him to the floor and stepped back, breathing hard, my pulse hammering in my temples. I swallowed, heard Reena shout again. Then I turned on the staircase light.

THREE

On the way to the hospital in the taxi, Reena said nothing, just stared through the window. After calling the cops, I had soaked a towel in warm water and wiped her face clean, then led her into the kitchen and made a cup of tea. She kept insisting she was "all right now," but her hands shook and she seemed distanced, as if she'd taken a couple of tranquillizers. She was able to tell me that Del was an ex-boyfriend. She had kicked him out a few years ago when she finally realized that he was never going to give up the booze and drugs. Tonight he had come back desperate for money and beaten her up when she refused to give him any.

After the cops had told Reena they'd be in touch to take her statement, they cuffed Del and took him away. Reena wouldn't let the cops radio for an ambulance, so I had called a cab and helped her get into some clothes, which she pulled on over her pajamas.

At the Queensway General Emergency ward we waited along with more than a dozen other people, sitting in hard plastic chairs. A wall-mounted TV was showing a tabloid news program. There were a few coffee tables littered with magazines, a couple of vending machines, a broken play centre for kids. An old man sat by himself, an IV tube snaking from the back of his hand to a bottle on a stand by his chair. A guy, groaning, his arm in a sling, was being comforted by a young woman.

I sat with Reena, my arm around her shoulder. She kept licking her swollen lip, her eyes darting to the door every few minutes, as if she expected Del to burst in and punch her around again.

"I'm thirsty," she croaked.

I bought two bottles of juice from the machine and turned back toward our chairs. Then I stopped. I saw Reena the way the strangers in the room must have viewed her. Under the harsh fluorescent lighting, her skin was dry and pale, the shiner on her left eye coming up purply-yellow, her swollen lip distorting her features. In her eyes was the glazed look of someone who still hadn't quite gotten a handle on what had happened.

And then Beth's face flashed into my mind, staring up at me from the library bench after I had hit her, with that same uncomprehending look on her startled face. As soon as it slithered into my mind, I tossed away the excuse that I had been justified. That had always been my defense. It's your own fault. You made me angry. You had it coming.

I was no different from the low-life I had almost thrown down the stairs.

———

Four hours later, a nurse in blue med fatigues came and led Reena away. I sat and waited, one of only a few uninjured, healthy people in a room full of casualties, until a different nurse brought her back a half-hour later. Reena's lip had been stitched up and a head bandage held an ice pack over her black eye.

"We've given her a sedative," the nurse told me, still holding Reena's arm. "Now, before we release her, this hospital has a strict protocol and I'm compelled to ask you some questions. Please follow me."

The nurse, a small, thin woman with jet-black hair and a no-nonsense manner, led us out of the room to a quiet spot in the hall. She released Reena's arm and adjusted the form attached to a clipboard.

"Have you reported this incident to the police?" she asked.

Reena nodded vaguely but said nothing. I told the nurse the cops had come to the café and taken away the man who had hit Reena. "One of them gave me his name and an incident number," I added, taking a piece of paper from my pocket. "The information is there."

The nurse nodded as she wrote. "Fine." Then she shook her head with disgust. "Sometimes I think we're living in a war zone. She's the third one tonight."

On the way home, Reena dozed, her head resting on my shoulder. I looked out the taxi window at the quiet, early morning streets, thinking about the day Cutter had taken my hands and examined my skinned knuckles. I knew now where he had been leading me when he left me his house and papers and personal history. He had wanted me to know why his hold on the real world was so weak, and why he had decided to do away with himself, and until tonight I had thought I understood. But there was more than that. His story was a mirror that showed me something about myself. He was telling me in his long, roundabout, Cutter fashion that when the darkness comes, from outside or from inside, and tempts you to mine the schoolyard, blow up the building, pick up the gun, throw the punch—then you have two choices, the green helmet or the blue one.

You can join the war, or you can keep the peace.

PART FOUR

PEACEKEEPING

Let us therefore put away the things of darkness,
and clothe ourselves in the armour of light.

—Saul of Tarsus, *Letter to the Romans*

ONE

I WAS BUSY AT the café for the next couple of weeks, taking on some of Reena's normal duties while she recuperated, so the home delivery service was suspended for a while. She wanted to stay out of sight until her shiner cleared up and her lip healed, she said. It was humiliating to be seen all banged up like she was. I asked her why she should be embarrassed. She was the victim. I know that, she replied. I still don't want to be seen.

Her battered face was a reminder of what I had discovered about myself, and what I had to do. I spent a lot of effort putting it off, telling myself how busy I was. On Sunday I slept in and puttered around my room for a while, killing time by cleaning the place up, but eventually I made my way down to Reena's kitchen with a bag of garbage and a half-dozen coffee mugs that had accumulated over the last week or so. I had tea and toast and jam with Reena while she watched a British soap opera centred around a bunch of losers who drank and gossiped at the same pub, then put on my jacket and told her I was going out.

"Where abouts?" she asked.

"Just something I gotta do," I said.

"Mr. Mysterious."

"That's me."

A while later I locked the tank to the rack outside the GO station and boarded the westbound train. While it rumbled along I tried to read, but couldn't concentrate. I lowered the book and looked out the window, fidgeting in my seat, watching factories and malls and housing tracts slip by as the train carried me closer and closer to Hamilton.

I wasn't very good at thinking things through. I had never been a planner. Most of the time I found what was happening in my life pretty confusing—sometimes scary— and trying to sort out my feelings and my actions was something I stayed clear of, the way you'd step around a puddle on your way down the sidewalk. Maybe, I thought, I had never wanted to look closely because I was afraid of what I'd see. Sitting in the swaying train car that day, lulled by the *click-clack, click-clack* of the wheels, I wondered if I had changed.

When I made my way though the Sunday crowd and out of the station, a bitter wind rushed from threatening clouds. April showers bring May flowers, I thought, a dumb rhyme we were taught in elementary school that was probably supposed to make us feel better. I buttoned my jacket and headed for the bus stop, fighting off the sense that I was sneaking into town against Carpino's orders.

The drizzle had begun by the time I stood in the parking lot across the road from Beth's house, a brick bungalow with a poured concrete stoop, just like all the other places on her street. I pulled up my collar against the rain, fighting the temptation to turn around and walk away.

I crossed the road and rang her bell. There was a big flowerpot against the iron railing, a dry twisted stalk sticking up from the dirt. Last year's geraniums, I thought, like Reena's. I pushed the bell again, just as the inner door opened.

Beth had cut her hair so that it was only a bit longer than mine, and the effect was to make her even prettier, even more feminine. Her navy warm-ups accentuated the light blue of her eyes. She had the friendliest, most open face I had ever seen, but when she realized who I was, her eyes went flat and she took a half step back into the vestibule. She stood there for a couple of seconds, watching me through the glass storm door.

Then she began to push the inner door closed.

"Wait!" I said.

She looked over her shoulder back into the house, then opened the storm door and put her head around.

"Don't come any closer," she said.

I backed up, holding the railing, took two steps down.

"My father's here," she said. "In the living room, right behind me. What do you want?"

"To tell you how sorry I am," I said. "To say I was wrong."

Slowly, she moved from behind the door onto the porch. She leaned back slightly, then tilted her head in the way I had always found so attractive, and moved her hand as if she was tucking a strand of hair behind her ear, only now her hair was too short.

"Coming here doesn't change anything," she said.

"I know."

"I could have charged you."

We stood silently for a few minutes. A car hissed by. Down the street, a kid yelled for his mother.

"I have to go now," Beth said, but she didn't move.

"Yeah, okay."

I took the last two steps and walked down her sidewalk. After I crossed the road, I turned. She was still standing on the porch in the rain, watching me.

On the train I saw the same factories and shopping centres slip past the window in reverse order. I didn't know what to think. I hadn't expected Beth to forgive me, to smile and bubble and say it didn't matter. I had been ready for anger, shouting, insults, anything but the cold brush-off I got. I was bugged by the fact that she hadn't appreciated my apology.

And at the same time I knew I had no right to expect anything more. I had to admit that I hadn't gone to her house for her sake. I had gone for me. To get back some self-respect. I can't say that I felt good about myself, but I didn't feel bad either, and that was something.

"You know what?" Reena said two nights later, laying down a book of four kings and discarding the three of clubs. "I think I'm gonna get a dog."

"You could throw away something useful once in a while," I complained. I picked up a card from the deck, glanced at it, and tossed it, disgusted, on the discard pile.

Reena was, to use her word, a builder in the card game she called Rummy. She laid down her books and straights as soon as she had collected them, accumulating points as the hand went along. I was a hoarder, keeping my points cards in my hand until I could slap them down all at once and go out on the discard. Showy but risky, because sometimes she went out first and left me with a mittful of losing cards.

"A dog? What for?"

"Oh, I don't know. I like dogs."

"First I've heard of it."

"Yeah, well, I have hidden depths," she said.

The truth probably was that she would feel safer with an animal around, after her scary experience with Del.

"What kind?" I asked.

"I don't know. I thought I'd take the bus up to the Humane Society near the Sherway tomorrow afternoon and see what they've got. Unless you'd rather not have a pet around the place."

"I like dogs," I replied, which was mostly true, I thought. I didn't really know.

The next afternoon I pedalled back to the café after a delivery and found Reena upstairs in her room, on her knees, making baby-talk to a caramel and white blob lying on a cushion in a wicker basket beside her easy chair. When it saw me, it jumped to its feet and began to pant. The stub on its rear end wiggled back and forth.

And I laughed.

"Stop," Reena said. "You'll hurt his feelings."

The dog had a smashed-in face and deep wrinkles that swooped from a spot over its glistening nose to the edges of its mouth, giving it a brainless smile. It stood less than knee height on bowed legs. One ear had been torn to a thin shred and one eye was missing, so that it seemed to be winking at me.

"He looks like a fighter," I said.

"I thought you two would have something in common."

"Very funny. Nobody's gonna steal him, anyway."

"That's what you said about the bike I got you, and look how good it turned out."

"This is the ugliest animal I've ever seen. I thought you wanted a dog for protection. *You'll* have to defend *him*."

"I felt sorry for him," Reena said, getting to her feet.

"I can understand why."

The dog made three circles in its bed, flopped down, and farted.

"I'm trying to think of a name for him," Reena said.

"How about Windy?"

She laughed.

"Or Patch, the One-Eyed Dog?"

"Yeah," Reena said. "Patch. I like that. Do you like your new name, Sweetie?" she cooed.

The dog began to snore.

One day, after I had dropped off Abe's lunch, I showed up at Lakshmi and Associates. Mrs. Smith was a ray of sunshine, as usual.

"Wonderful to see you again," she muttered as she rammed a pencil into the electric sharpener mounted on her desk.

I waited until the whine died away. "I need to see Lakshmi."

She made a big show of blowing sawdust from the tip of her pencil before running her bony finger down the open page of an appointment calendar.

"I'm awfully sorry. I don't see you booked for today."

"Probably because I'm not."

"Well, then—"

"Lakshmi told me to come any time. No advance notice needed."

"Indeed."

"Indeed, indeed."

Lakshmi looked better than ever that afternoon. She greeted me with a wide smile.

"Hi, Lee. Come on in."

"Just wanted to see you for a minute," I said.

She laughed. "Take a seat, and take your time."

I sat down. Cleared my throat. "It's about this money that Cutter left me."

She nodded.

"Well, can I get at it any time?"

"Sure. How much do you need?"

"I'm not sure yet."

"Okay. When you know, call and I'll arrange it. How would you like it? Cash? Or I can arrange a direct deposit to your bank account."

"I don't have a bank account."

Her head tilted slightly to the side. "You don't—well, no problem. What about a money order? You can cash it anywhere."

"Can you send money to someone else's account?"

"Easy as pie. I just need the name and number. What's this all about?"

"Um . . ."

She held up her hand. "Never mind. I shouldn't have asked."

"Thanks, Lakshmi. I'll let you know."

"See you, then," she said.

I got up and headed for the door. Then I had a thought.

"If I ever needed a lawyer," I blurted out, "could it be you?"

"Why on earth would you need legal representation?"

"I don't know. I was just thinking."

"What, you were scooting past the office on your bike and suddenly decided you required a hired gun?" she laughed.

"Well . . ."

"Have you robbed a bank or something?"

"Nope."

"Didn't murder anyone before breakfast, did you?"

"Not today."

Her smile fell away. "Lee, is something wrong?"

"No, nothing's wrong. I just wondered."

She came out from behind the desk and held out her left hand, palm up.

"Got a buck in your pocket?"

I fished out a coin and handed it to her. She closed her fist on it and held out her other hand. We shook.

"You just hired yourself a lawyer," she said.

TWO

REENA HUNG THE CLOSED sign on the door as I was sweeping up after the lunch crowd.

"Can I have the rest of the day off?" I asked. "I got something I need to do."

"Why not do it Sunday when we're closed?"

"Because."

"Will you be back to help with dinner?"

"I don't know."

"My, aren't you a fountain of information today."

"I do my best."

"Hmmm," Reena said.

For the second time that month I hopped the train to Hamilton, then climbed aboard a city bus. The neighbourhood where I had grown up looked the same—drab and defeated, streets with low-rise apartment buildings, discount and variety stores, FOR RENT signs in empty shop windows. The run-down building where I used to live stood between two identical sand-coloured structures, each with a cracked concrete sidewalk leading to the front doors and a lawn that had barely survived winter. I got out my key, let myself in, and rode the creaky elevator to the third floor. In the hall outside number four I stopped, kicked off my boots—I didn't want to leave any sign that I had been there—and listened, my ear against the door.

My father had never missed a day's work. He'd be at the garage, stretched out under a car or leaning in under the hood, wielding a wrench. But I wanted to be sure.

I unlocked the door and stepped inside. I smelled burnt toast and warmed-over pizza. Sections of a newspaper were strewn across the couch beside a take-out pizza box. A TV program listing lay open on the floor next to my father's easy chair, the remote resting on top. I padded on stocking feet into the kitchen, where a radio played quietly. My father thought the sound of the radio discouraged burglars. A bowl and cup sat in the sink beside a pot sticky with oatmeal.

I pulled open the drawer where he kept his bills and bank book and credit card receipts. He hadn't gotten any neater since I saw him last. I removed the drawer and placed it on the table, pulling up a chair.

I had seen him dozens of times sitting where I was now, a calculator and pencil close at hand, shaking his head and muttering, "I just can't seem to get anywhere with this. No matter what I do, I'm always behind." Then he'd take a pull on his beer, set it down with a thump, pick up the pencil, and begin punching numbers into the calculator, as if making another run at the calculations would change something.

It took me a few minutes to paw through the clutter and find what I was looking for. I scanned the figures and jotted down the numbers I wanted on a piece of paper, then replaced the drawer.

While I was in the apartment, I took a look around. His bed was unmade, the closet door open, loose change on the dresser top beside the matching brush and comb my mother had bought him for Christmas one year. I picked up the brush. If she had still been alive, my mother would have been almost ten years older, now. But I could only remember her the way she was back then, frozen in time while her little boy grew up without her.

In my room, some school books sat unopened on my plywood desk. My bed was neatly made up, the room tidy, as if he expected me home any minute. I stood in the doorway, wishing I could stay. Just hang up my jacket and turn on the TV and wait for him to come home. Maybe send out for a tub of chicken, shoot the breeze while we ate, then watch a ball game together.

I pulled on my boots in the hall, and took the elevator back down to the street.

As the train passed the Oakville station, I keyed a number into my cell.

"Smith and Associates."

"It's Lee," I said.

"Is it indeed?" Mrs. Smith sniffed.

"I need to talk to Lakshmi."

"I beg your pardon. I can hardly hear you."

"I'm on the train," I said, and repeated my message.

"Let me see if she's available to speak."

A moment later Mrs. Smith came back on the line. "She'll be with you in a moment. Please hold. Don't hang up."

"I won't hang—"

But she cut me off. Got me again, I thought. I fished the piece of paper from my pocket.

A few minutes later, I heard Lakshmi's voice. "Hello, Lee."

"I got those numbers for you," I said, and read them to her.

"Okay, Lee. Consider it done."

A week later, when I hauled myself bleary-eyed from bed and clumped down the stairs for my Sunday morning coffee in Reena's kitchen, I heard voices before I reached the bottom stair. In the hall outside the kitchen, I turned back toward my room. I stopped, took a deep breath. When I entered the kitchen the voices fell silent.

My father sat across from Reena, a mug of coffee on the table in front of him. I poured myself a cup and leaned back against the counter. Watched closely by Patch the One-Eyed Dog, Reena spooned blueberry jam onto a piece of toast and spread it around, holding the toast on her finger tips, so the jam covered the whole surface. I had told her once that she ate like a kid.

"I'm young at heart," she had said.

I eyed my father over the rim of my mug. In the morning light he looked pale and tired, his dark hair limp, his face creased. He had missed a couple of spots when he shaved. Thick fingers curled around his cup, the nails not quite free of grease from the garage.

"Morning, Lee," Reena said before she bit into her toast.

My father nodded. "Hi," I said to him.

He pulled a piece of paper from his shirt pocket, unfolded it, and spread it out on the table with his palms. Reena picked up her cup and plate.

"Time to get dressed," she said to no one.

I didn't want her to leave, but my father spoke first. "Stick around for a little, okay?" he said. "The last two times Lee and me talked, we needed a referee."

Reena slumped back into her chair and pulled her bathrobe together at her throat.

"Sit down, Lee," my father said, pointing to the third chair.

"No, thanks. I'll stay here."

"See?" he said to Reena. "Defiance. I haven't said a word and already—"

Reena's voice was harsh. "Look, Doug. It's been a long week. The last thing I need on my day off is to listen to you two bang away at each other. Lee, would it kill you to sit down? Jesus, the two of you are like a couple of infants."

I did as she asked. My father looked at the paper, as if he was memorizing the numbers.

"Funny thing happened a couple of days ago, Reena. My bank statement came in the mail. I left it a couple of days before I opened it. No use hurrying the bad news, eh? When I got around to looking at it, the statement showed a balance of zero for my loan. The bank made a mistake, I figured, deposited a bunch of money in the wrong account."

Reena said nothing. She picked up her knife and ran the point back and forth across her plate.

My father continued to stare at the paper in front of him and talk to Reena. "I called them from work the next day. They said it wasn't a mistake. The money came in from another bank by electronic transfer. I told them I didn't know anything about it. So on my lunch hour I went over there. They said the money was sent from a bank in New Toronto."

He looked up, at Reena. "I thought to myself, only one person I know in New Toronto. Only one person I know who would give me that kind of money. My sister."

Reena shook her head. "I never sent you a cent," she said, putting down the knife and reaching into her bathrobe pocket for her cigarettes. She lit up and blew a cloud toward the ceiling.

"Then," my father went on, as if he hadn't heard her, "I realized that this here mysterious electronic transfer was exactly the balance I owed. Somebody knew to the penny how much it would take to clear the loan. Sure is strange, eh, Reena?"

"A mystery," she said, and glanced at me.

"I went home a while ago," I said to my father, "and looked at your records."

He was silent for a moment, taking in the information.

"Where the hell could you come up with that kind of money?" he demanded. "Thousands of bucks. You stole it, didn't you?"

"A friend of mine left it to me in his will."

"What? Left it— Who?"

"I told you. A friend. His name is—was—Bruce Cutter."

A crease formed on my father's brow. He scratched his head. Looked at Reena, who nodded.

"He's telling the truth, Doug."

"A friend," he said.

"Yeah."

"An older guy?"

"Yeah."

Then his eyes widened. "Jesus, Lee, you're not telling me you're—"

Reena threw back her head and let out a laugh that rattled the dishes in the sink and brought on a coughing fit.

"What's so goddam funny?" my father said, his fingers crumpling the paper.

When she could breathe again, Reena said, still laughing, "It's just that, if you saw the way Lee looks at the college girls in the morning, you wouldn't think what you're thinking."

"Look, it's no big deal," I explained. "I wanted to give you some money. To get rid of that loan you've been carrying around since. . . . So you can quit your second job. That's all."

He looked out the window, then down at his hands, then at the bank statement. Quietly, Reena left the room. I heard her bedroom door close softly.

"No big deal, you tell me," he whispered. "I don't know what to say."

"You don't have to say anything."

"I can't accept it."

My hands began to tremble. Then came the rush, the blast of anger, the heat rising into my face. The words burst out before I could think. "Why the hell not?"

Then I looked at his rough hands, his thick fingers, the skin raw from solvents he used to dissolve oil and grease. His face, pinched from too much hard labour and too much worry. And I realized something I had never seen, because I had never looked. He was lonely. He worked twelve hours a day, shuffled from home to work and back, slept, and then did it all again. For him, tomorrow was nothing but another today.

"It . . ." he began, then faltered. "Try to understand, Lee. The vacation your mom and me took, it was all I could give her. She was sick and she was gonna die, and I couldn't do anything about that. But I could take her to the places she had always wanted to visit. You shoulda seen her over there in Italy, at the galleries and that. She knew she didn't have long, but she was full of—joy. Only regret she had, she'd say, was that you weren't there.

"See, the loan I'm working to pay back, it's like I'm still doing it for her. I can still give her something. I know it sounds crazy, but if I take your money, I'll lose that." He rubbed the back of his hand under his nose and took a swallow of coffee. "Does that make any sense?"

I sat back in my chair, turning my cup around and around by the handle, thinking. I understood what he was telling me.

"Yeah, Dad, it does," I said. "But think about it this way. When Mom got sick, I was just a little kid. You took her to the museums and art galleries. But what could I do for her? Nothing. I haven't been a very good son. This is my chance. I want to do this for both of you."

We were silent for a few minutes. Then my father said, "I haven't heard that word for a long time."

"What word?"

"You called me Dad."

He hung his head. "I miss her," he said. "I miss both of you."

THREE

I WAS HALFWAY THROUGH a breakfast of bacon and eggs when a stranger shambled through the café door—a not-very-tall guy, wearing an overcoat that hung almost to his broken-down running shoes, a greasy baseball cap and a scarf wrapped around his neck and over his ears, although the sun was shining out on Lakeshore Boulevard. A street person who had heard about Reena's, I guessed.

He made his way to the back counter just as the Queen of Sweden turned away, holding her mug of steaming Colombian. She gave him a look that said, They're letting just anyone in here nowadays, and took a seat at her table. Even from my booth I could see the man's hands shaking as he picked up a mug. If he tried filling it, he'd burn himself for sure. I hustled over, beating him to the coffee pot, and topped up my own mug.

"Can I pour some for you, too?" I asked.

Silently, he handed me his cup. His eyes were red-rimmed and watery, his complexion waxy under a few days' greying stubble. His mouth had collapsed in on itself. No teeth, I guessed.

"Cream and sugar?" I asked.

He nodded, sniffed wetly, and jammed his hands in his coat pockets to hide the tremors.

"Grab a seat and I'll bring it over to you."

He hesitated, then did as I suggested. I put in three spoons of sugar and lots of cream. Sometimes the only nourishment the alkies got all day was what came in their coffee, Reena had told me one time.

He was sitting at a table by himself, his back straight, chin up, staring straight ahead. He looked almost dignified. I set the mug down on the table in front of him.

"How about something to eat?" I asked. "We're out of cookies, but I could get you something."

He looked up, nodded, wrapped his soiled hands around the mug, then carefully, as if lifting a piece of priceless china, raised it shakily to his mouth. He slurped, swallowed, and said, "Ah."

I headed for the kitchen, and noticed Reena leaning in the doorway, arms crossed, watching me and smiling.

"What?" I said, following her through.

She quickly made a honey sandwich, slipped it onto a plate and handed it to me. "Let's hope he can keep it down," she said.

"Why were you watching me?" I asked.

"Oh, I was just thinking."

"Thinking what?"

"Nothing."

I pushed open the kitchen door. "Tough guy," she added, as I passed through.

I put the plate down beside the guy's cup, then went back to my booth.

Because it was Sunday, I had phoned ahead to make sure I'd find Sergeant Carpino at the cop shop. When I asked for him at the front desk, the officer on duty picked up her phone, punched a number, mumbled something, and said, "He'll be with you in a minute."

I waited on one of the benches. The place was pretty quiet. A few uniforms came and went. A phone rang somewhere. After a while Carpino, his shirt sleeves rolled up above the elbow, his tie pulled loose, came through a door beside the desk. He stood with his hands on his hips and looked at the duty cop, who pointed to me.

I stood and walked over to him.

"Long time," he said.

"Yeah."

"You weren't supposed to come back here."

"I need to talk to you."

"Still living in New Toronto? With your aunt?"

"Yeah."

"Your dad know you're here?"

"No. This isn't about him."

Carpino looked me over. "What's it like out?"

"Sunny. Warm."

"Let's take a walk."

He retrieved his jacket from the squad room and led me out of the station and down the block to a micro-park next to a parking arcade. Pigeons strutted around on the dirty sidewalk next to potted shrubs, their heads bobbing, scurrying out of the way when a pedestrian came by.

Carpino sat on a bench and lit up a smoke. "So, what's going on?" he asked.

I sat next to him. "I want to know if you're going to charge me," I said.

He gave me a suspicious look. "Explain."

"That day you dropped me off at my aunt's in New Toronto, you told me if I came back home you'd nail me for the B and E and a couple of assaults."

"Yeah, so?"

"So I have to know, are you going to charge me? Because, if you are, I want you to do it now. I'm ready. I have a lawyer. If you're not, I need to know that, too. I don't want all this hanging over my head."

Carpino watched the pigeons for a moment, then seemed to find something fascinating in the traffic light across the way. "You seem . . . different," he said.

"I am different."

"How so?"

"It's a long story. Look, I want to start over," I said. "But I want to pay my bills first, you know?"

"So you came here to be arrested. To turn yourself in."

"If that's what it takes, yeah."

He lit a fresh cigarette off the old one, dropped the butt onto the pavement, and ground it out with the toe of his shoe. One of the pigeons strutted over to investigate. Stuffing the pack of smokes into his shirt pocket, Carpino looked me straight in the eye, his lips a thin line.

"I don't know nothing about any assaults or a B and E," he said.

"What do you mean?"

He stood and pointed toward the nearest intersection. "See that sign for the city bus?"

"Yeah."

"When number 52 comes along, you get on it. It'll take you right to the GO station."

He turned and walked back along the street, toward the police station.

FOUR

ON THE SATURDAY OF the July 1 holiday weekend, I steered the tank into the driveway of the house on 13th Street, parked and locked it in the garage, and walked around to the front, carrying a bag of books I had picked up at the library. Clancy had gotten me onto the Rebus detective novels, and I was reading them in order.

Reena was sprawled on a chaise longue in the shade of the verandah, smoking and reading a movie magazine, a beer on the table beside her. Patch the One-Eyed Dog lay beside her snoring.

Cutter's mailbox had been removed, the surveillance camera taken down, and the verandah freshly painted. Reena had put in a flower garden across the front of the house, with a cedar tree at each end. Patch peed on the trees whenever he could.

I mounted the steps, plunked my bag down on the table, and took a swig of her beer. It was icy cold.

"Ahh," I said. "Boy, it's hot out. Abe says we're going to have a banger of a thunderstorm later."

"Tell that to the hired help," she said, waving toward my father.

He was on his hands and knees beside a wheelbarrow, smoothing the veins of new cement between sections of the flagstone path. His T-shirt and jeans were smeared with mortar. He had re-sodded the lawn and it stretched green and weedless to the sidewalk.

"Do you think he'll ever stop working?" I asked.

"He's never owned a house before," she said. "He's bubbling over with enthusiasm. Watching him makes me want to go and lie down for a while."

"You are lying down," I said.

"Good point."

At the beginning of the summer I had gone to Lakshmi and asked her to transfer the house to my father's name. When all the paperwork had been done, I had mailed it to him with a note saying, "Now you have to move to New Toronto."

"Be patient," Reena had advised me. "He's a proud man. He has to get used to the idea of being given something."

He had quit his job at the department store by then, but couldn't tear himself away from the apartment where he and my mother and I had once been a family. It had taken a few weeks and a lot of phone calls, with Reena helping me nag, to persuade him to move to 13th Street. It wasn't long before he found a job at a local garage. His old employer had given him a good reference.

Together, my father and I had repainted every room in the house. He moved into Cutter's old bedroom, and I took the "crazy room," after we had replaced the painted-over window and papered the walls. I had moved up the computer equipment I wanted and given the rest away. I held onto two of Cutter's aluminum disks and hung them in my window, for old time's sake. Cutter's office was our living room. We kept the big TV, but got rid of the satellite dishes.

My father and Reena were pushing hard to get me to go back to school, but so far I had resisted. "I don't have time," I said. Which was true. The Lee Mercer Courier Service was busier than ever and I still helped Reena at the café. "Maybe I'll take a correspondence course or something," I told them, mostly to keep them off my back. But when I thought about it, it wasn't such a bad idea.

I went inside the house, pulled a cold beer from the fridge and took it back to the verandah.

"Dad," I called. "Time for a break."

He stood, wiped his brow, dropped the trowel into the wheelbarrow, and joined my aunt and me. He was tanned from working outdoors and his eyes had lost their beaten-down look. He dropped into a chair, took a long pull from the bottle, and sighed.

"You know," he said. "We oughtta plant perennials in the back yard. Less maintenance."

"Annuals are better," Reena said lazily.

While they argued good-naturedly, I sat on the steps and looked up and down 13th Street. Between the houses opposite I caught a glimpse of the lawns and maple trees in the big park that used to be a mental hospital, and I remembered Cutter telling me he liked to visit once in a while and commune with the ghosts of the patients who used to live there. He had gone to a violent, far-off place to make peace, and he had brought the war home with him, in his mind, a bloodless wound deeper than any bullet could go. I looked at our new grass and stone path, breathed in the odour of fresh paint, and tried to remember him, not as I had last seen him, but as the guy with racing cars on his pajamas and a stack of printouts in his filing cabinet, beside his blue helmet. My friend, who showed me that I had to face the war inside myself before I could find peace.

AUTHOR'S NOTE

The Blue Helmet is a work of fiction, and all characters are products of my imagination. Any resemblance to real persons is entirely coincidental. The firefight between Canadian UNPROFOR forces and elements of the Croatian army in the "Medak Pocket" on September 16, 1993, is a matter of record. I have made certain changes in the details of that action and the subsequent events in order to serve my narrative.

I found the following useful in researching background for this story:

Carol Off. *The Ghosts of Medak Pocket.* Toronto: Random House Canada, 2004.

Lee A. Windsor. "The Medak Pocket." www.cda-cdai.ca/library/medakpocket.htm

John R. Lampe. "Ethnic Politics and the End of Yugoslavia," the final chapter of his *Yugoslavia as History*. Cambridge: Cambridge University Press, 1996.

Readers who are skeptical of Bruce Cutter's reluctance to fire his weapon even in the heat of an attack are invited to consult Gwynne Dyer's *War*, Toronto: Random House Canada, 2004, pp. 54–7, and pp. 5–39 of Dave Grossman's *On Killing: The Psychological Cost of Learning to Kill in War and Society*. Toronto: Little, Brown, 1995.

ACKNOWLEDGEMENTS

I want to thank my publisher, Maya Mavjee, for support-
ing this project; my editor, Amy Black; and my friend and
agent, John Pearce.

As always I am grateful to my support group, Dylan,
Megan and Brendan Bell; and especially Ting-xing Ye for
her encouragement and inspiration.

Special thanks to Sloba Golubovich-Bray for advice in
cultural matters.

ABOUT THE AUTHOR

William Bell's young adult novels have been translated into nine languages and have won many awards, among them the Ruth Schwartz Award for Excellence, the Belgium Award for Excellence, the Manitoba Young Readers' Choice Award, the Mr. Christie's Award, and the Canadian Library Association Young Adult Book of the Year Award. William Bell lives in Orillia, Ontario with author Ting-xing Ye.